Once again Claudia felt paralyzed by the conflicting responses of anger and dread. She simply nodded that she understood. Sameera rose and sat next to Claudia on the fountain wall. Delicately, she lifted the strands of Claudia's hair that were caught underneath the leather collar, moved the chain out of the way, and begin to brush. After days of being tugged and ignored, led and shunned, poked and forgotten, after days of strange confinement, Sameera's attention to her hair—the little jabs of pain at snarls and the full, rhythmic strokes in between—was an ecstasy of attention. Soon Claudia closed her eyes and was some place else, remembering the hundreds of times Martha had done this for her. Not even the snugness of the ribbons that bound her hands or the heavy smell of incense or the shrill music that went on and on from the other side of the doomed room could break this moment of unexpected peace. Claudia rolled her head with Sameera's strokes, even though the collar rubbed roughly against her skin. She felt her body begin to sway underneath the soft abayya, felt her hardened nipples dip into little pools of the cool fabric.

ACROSS

BLUE DAWSON

Genesis Press Inc.

Le Marais

An imprint of Genesis Press Inc.
Publishing Company

Genesis Press, Inc.
P.O. Box 101
Columbus, MS 39703

All characters in this book have no existence outside the imagination of the author and have no relation whatsoever to anyone
bearing the same name or names. They are not even distantly
inspired by any individual known or unknown to the author and
all incidents are pure invention.

ISBN: 1-58571-149-7
Manufactured in the United States of America

First Edition

Visit us at www.genesis-press.com
or call at 1-888-Indigo-1

DEDICATION

To Linda, who forever is my Martha.

ACKNOWLEDGMENTS

"Thank you to the women in North Africa who took me into the odas and souks and let me see faces behind the veils."

PART I

SEA

CHAPTER 1

Finding a freighter, one that would book a few passengers for a tramp across the Atlantic or some other ocean was just about impossible. But the idea had seemed perfect: nothing to do except take an occasional meal with the captain, read, rest in fair seas on deck, portside out, starboard side home. They would be an intimate group of two. No fancy balls, just a suitcase full of books, Scrabble, their laptop computers, and a case of good Scotch. Two cases of good Scotch.

Martha Bekele and Claudia Simmerhorn, lovers too long separated because of the complications of careers, had spoken to travel agents, had looked up freighter companies in the San Francisco, Los Angeles, and New York *Yellow Pages*, had even asked for referrals from tugboat companies. One brochure featured the superstructure of an oil tanker "where two hundred passengers can enjoy companionship and fiestas high above the sea." Another picture in the same brochure showed a lounge where elderly couples danced to "disco one night, old favorites the next."

Nothing seemed right until Martha saw a small advertisement in the back of the *Vogue* she was reading while having her hair done at Medusa's, an exclusive salon in North Beach.

Worldwide Travel by Freighter
Leisurely, Slow Travel to the World's Ports
Call (701) 674-3210

She ripped the page out and wouldn't even trust it to the depths of her bag. When her hair was done, she carried the advertisement out to the Mercedes and put it on the passenger seat where it couldn't possibly be lost on the way home.

Martha had to wait until the next morning to get someone to answer the number. A week later a computer printout arrived, with handwritten annotations, listing sailings through 2003. It was a short list:

Port	Destination	Sailing	Name/Registry
Oakland	Seattle	11/01	Sea Star/Canada
Oakland	Taiwan	1/02	Cronos/Liberia
Oakland	Port of Spain, Trinidad	2/02	Capricorn/Panama
New York	Lisbon, Portugal	1/03	Bengal Star/Uruguay
Boston	Izmir, Turkey	4/03	Swan II/Liberia
Long Beach	Chittagong, Bangladesh	4/03	Pacific Star/Haiti

Martha made inquiries about the Swan II. The agency told her it was small, clean freighter owned by an Indian shipping company. It had a mostly Greek crew and was scheduled on this trip to have a "mixed cargo." Specifications would be sent shortly.

An 8 X 10 manila clasp envelope arrived the following Tuesday with gross tonnage figures, two loose Polaroids, one of the inside of a cabin, another of the "dining area." The enclosed note said that in late October the boat would be in Bath, Maine for minor refitting, and that Martha and Claudia were welcome to tour her before "a deposit became non-refundable."

Both Martha and Claudia had almost weekly business obligations in New York, and they decided that they could meet there, fly to Boston, and then make the drive up to Maine to see what the Swan II looked like.

One cloudy day in late October they negotiated their way out of Boston's horrible downtown traffic in their rental car, Martha behind the wheel and Claudia navigating. Traffic thinned as they drove through New Hampshire and by the time they crossed into Maine, they were almost the only car on the road. The maps were folded and put away and they relaxed, enjoying the ride along Route 1A which meandered through the reds and oranges of a New England fall, past lobster boat harbors along the edges of gray, clapboard villages. They stopped at a clam shack for steamers and a produce stand for McIntosh apples, and felt blessed to be together in the hush of a wet autumn.

When they arrived at the Bath shipyards it was evening. Martha gave their letter of introduction to the security guard who directed them to drive between two warehouses and park at the edge of the dock. An aircraft carrier was moored directly in front of them. The sparks from welding torches fell from its superstructure onto the immense deck. Along side the carrier was a destroyer; the women watched as a crane lowered its giant hook to grab part of a gun turret on its bow. There were other navy ships end to end along the docks and some anchored our further, huge dark forms against the darkening sky. But there was no freighter named the Swan II.

They got back in the rental car, disappointed and cold. Martha had just picked up her cell phone to make an angry call when they heard a ship's horn blow twice. Because it seemed insistent and several octaves too high to have come from the naval ships, Martha and Claudia got out of the car and looked over the edge of the dock into the water. There, squeezed underneath the stern of the aircraft carrier, was a launch. The pilot, clearly expecting them, took a cigar out of his mouth and impatiently waved them aboard.

Martha and Claudia carefully climbed down a steel ladder and with the help of the pilot's oily hand, leapt on board the launch. They motored out into the river through the canyons of giant gray hulls and there, tucked in like a forgotten bathtub toy, was the Swan II.

Martha looked to Claudia and grinned. The ship had a hospital-white superstructure, shiny black hull, and a bright red Plimsoll line. There was no rust, no peeling paint, nothing corroded or sea worn. Nowhere on deck were piggyback cargo containers, those unromantic aluminum trailers that made ships look like railroad flatcars.

For Martha it was a child's version of a freighter, a perfect image, simple, clean, uncomplicated. She was grabbed Claudia's elbow to pull her closer and whispered, "Can you imagine how wonderfully alone we're going to be?"

Claudia smiled back at her lover. "Yes," she said. "I wish we could start right now."

The launch idled beside to a float attached to the Swan II by a steep, flexible gangway, and after another perilous transfer and climb, Martha and Claudia were on board. A security guard in a heavy coat perfunctorily saluted their arrival on deck and then led them on a tour. He showed them six passenger cabins, two on B deck and four up on A deck. Theirs would be a small two-room suite on the lower deck. The sitting room had two over-stuffed reading chairs, a floor lamp, and a coffee table. The bedroom was just big enough for two double beds with a small bedside chest between them. The bathroom was the size of a phone booth but there was room enough for a shower stall and a countertop for toiletries.

In spite of the metal walls, the low ceilings, and the numerous pipes overhead, the suite was cozy; the plush taupe rug and celedon tinted walls seemed to offer repose, relaxation, and the opportunity for reflection. On the spot Martha and Claudia decided to commit themselves to the non-refundable deposit, and, better still, to setting sail.

A month later they received a letter from Worldwide Travel by Freighter.

We must inform you of special circumstances that have arisen and may affect your decision to travel with us on the Swan II. As you know the Swan II can accommodate twelve passengers in six cabins. While we normally provide our clients with a passenger list so they have a head start in forming what often become lasting friendships, we have been asked not to release the names of those on this sailing. We can tell you that all four cabins on A deck have been reserved for Prince Jed al Hann who has contracted us to provide comfort and security for four of his family members and staff to Algeria.

The Swan II has added Ghazaouet, Algeria, as a port of call for their convenience, although for political reasons we cannot allow on-shore tour visits for you.

The Prince has requested that his family be assured absolute privacy at all times. They are to eat alone, be attended only by their own cook and domestic staff, and not be exposed to socializing.

We can accommodate this request by securing A deck for the Prince's family and reserving the dining room for their use. You would still have complete access to the lounge/library and the rest of the ship's decks.

We can assure you that you would be quite comfortable on the Swan II in spite of these circumstances, but we also understand that the chance to make new friends with us is one of the reasons people choose intimate freighter travel. We will be happy to give you a full refund and a discount on one of our future trips.

Please let us know of your decision as soon as possible.

With apologies,

Ty Sanderson, President

Eastern Crescent Lines

Ty Sanderson had not needed to apologize. Seclusion from the other passengers was not an imposition but a blessing to Martha and Claudia, further evidence that the trip would be a perfect escape from their busy lives.

Martha Bekele was the most aggressive partner of a successful advertising agency. It was lucrative but burnout work. Not only was she an anomaly as a Black woman in a mostly white, male-dominated cutthroat business, Martha had the ironic disadvantage of being gorgeous, of constantly having to erect barriers against the salacious fantasies of her colleagues. Martha, now in her early forties, purposely presented a no-nonsense exterior. Her black hair was short, worn close to her head and smoothed with gel. She favored tailored suits with skirts that came just below the knee and jackets that buttoned almost to her collarbone. Martha sought to intimidate her admirers, not to encourage them, and she generally succeeded in her endeavor.

Claudia Simmerhorn, Martha's partner, was formerly a writer for W2. She'd recently resigned her post, no longer able to tolerate the swish of satin on anorexic, disdainful eighteen year-old models. She had written the last column she would ever have to write about haute couture, the hot new color of the season, and "daring asymmetrical hemlines," and for the moment, didn't even care about finding another career. Claudia was tired, though her weariness showed only in her eyes. She, too, was a natural beauty, and though she, too, tried to hide her resemblance to the public's idealized sense of beauty, her efforts were generally in vain. She was embarrassed by the superficiality of glamour and didn't want to be noticed by anyone other than Martha, but even with big dark glasses and her long, silky brown hair shoved up into a Yankees cap, Claudia was the object of general attention. She was simply too tall to be inconspicuous, too elegant for refuge in the shapeless, black cotton sweaters she favored.

Martha's rejection of social expectations was one of the things Claudia liked best about her, right from the start. And Claudia's indifference to her physical beauty was one of the things that drew Martha to her from the very first.

Martha and Claudia had met at Radcliff, two bright, aggressive young women who had been lovers and then who had tried not to be lovers through marriages and separate continents and hungers that had driven them to their respective largely unhappy successes.

For reasons she never quite understood, Martha married an investor who worked for the World Bank in Asia. For four years she pretended to be happy or pretended that to be happy didn't matter. But at night, every night, whether with her husband in Tokyo or at her Pacific Heights home in San Francisco, it was the memory of Claudia that made her ache with loneliness. One day Martha realized that her career and her marriage were simply diversions, blankets thrown over her head to keep the monster of longing away, and that she no longer wanted to pretend.

Claudia had been easy to find. Her name was on the masthead of W2; she moved conspicuously between New York and Paris; she kept a thoroughbred in Virginia. She had had a husband who was a Fifth Avenue psychiatrist and a barroom drunk; wisely, she had gotten rid of him. And like Martha, she had been waiting.

That was ten years before. Since then Martha and Claudia had been devoted partners, but separated far too often. Now, aboard the Swan II, the women believed they would find a perfect world alone and with each other.

CHAPTER 2

By the time the taxi was loaded with their many pieces of luggage, every bell hop at the Boston Regency Hotel had been in on the spectacle, offering help, a space-saving idea, stares that were amazed and kind and admiring. It was the way almost a month of isolation at sea should begin, with affirmation that what the two women were leaving behind was, indeed, worth leaving behind.

The taxi pulled out onto Port Street, merged into heavy traffic, and almost sideswiped a truck that advertised "Hemingway's Seafood" over a picture of a trawler in a heavy sea. The women simultaneously sought each other's hand and then Martha said with as much disbelief as assertion, "We've done it. We've really done it."

Claudia looked at her lover. They were just moments into the long-awaited escape, and already she was beginning to feel safe, innocent, almost like a girl again. She hardly wanted to risk speaking, to risk saying anything beyond, "We've begun something wonderful."

CHAPTER 3

"I help you all trip. Those other guests not want me, so now I take care of just you. Lucky for all of us, huh?"

When Martha had first opened the cabin door, she was immediately reminded of the possums that used to frequent her grandmother's garden in rural Georgia. But this possum was wearing an immaculate white uniform and introduced himself as Nikkos, their steward.

Martha nodded and the man went on. "Lucky for me, I guess they no like Greeks, but why come on this ship then? We all Greeks and Filipinos, except Captain and first mate."

The man was about sixty, short, and had a pallid, oily complexion. Martha couldn't help but notice how his eyes seemed to darken and withdraw into narrow slits and then, as if catching themselves at something nasty, widen suddenly with civility. The habit disturbed her. It was late in the afternoon and after the taxi ride and the formalities of boarding the ship, she was tired and in no mood for this strange man's prattle.

Martha extended her hand as if she were throwing a jab. "Nikkos," she said curtly, "I'm Ms. Bekele and this is my companion, Ms. Simmerhorn."

Claudia nodded at the man before returning to pulling at the fingers of her kid gloves.

"We are very pleased to meet you," Martha continued, "and trust that you will find us for the most part self-sufficient passengers. However, we would appreciate your bringing our luggage as soon as possible, and then perhaps one or two things can be done in our suite."

Martha knew her words sounded like a rehearsed speech; she also knew that formality allowed few cracks through which familiarity could slip. She did not want the obligation of having to chat with this disturbing little man for the next four weeks.

For a moment the man's eyes darkened and narrowed. Martha resisted a shudder. "I be right back with hand truck," he said then. "After we leave port, captain would like to introduce himself. We can arrange time?"

Martha stepped forward, effectively pushing him back through the door with her will. "Yes," she said, "that might be pleasant. Goodbye."

The door closed and it was suddenly very quiet in the little suite. Claudia had finished removing her gloves and had found a towel to wipe the condensation off the porthole glass. The porthole looked onto the gray harbor: cranes, two fireboats, several brick waterfront buildings behind, rain. Not much else. Martha was suddenly intensely aware that they inhabited the fragile moment between two lives. Soon, intensity would be replaced by inactivity, the larger world by the solitary confinement of their little rooms.

Claudia turned the giant wing nuts that latched the porthole shut and swung it open, almost, Martha thought, as if testing for possible escape. Cold, damp air rushed into the room and Claudia quickly closed the porthole again. When she turned around, Martha was there. She removed Claudia's wool hat and began to stroke her long hair loose. Claudia bowed her head to the lovely, caressing fingers. She wanted the moment to last forever.

"Martha?" Claudia whispered. "Do you remember that time you were in Hong Kong and I couldn't reach you, not by phone or by email?"

Martha continued to stroke Claudia's hair. "Yes," she whispered back, "that was a bad time."

"No, it was worse than a bad time. I wasn't sure I could have lasted much longer without hearing from you. Please, don't let's ever be apart again."

Before Martha could reply there was a loud knock on the door. With a sigh of frustration Martha left Claudia and jerked open the door.

It was Nikkos. "I bring your things now," he said, indicating the women's luggage stacked behind him. "Other people still not on board. You have plenty of time before we sail. Entire dining room changed, some tables gone, some big chairs moved in, pillows on floor. Captain himself, Captain tell me, 'Stay out, Nikkos.' He not nice about it." Martha heard both anger and wonder in the man's voice. "I do this for twenty-two years, never see deck and cabins secret. Strange and strange."

"Nikkos," Martha said, resisting the unusual urge to be curious, "before you bring in the bags, do you suppose you could get us some ice?"

Again the man's eyes darkened before he abruptly turned and closed the door.

The women's little suite was hopelessly cluttered with luggage and Claudia's cello. Claudia despaired; she was certain that they would need the rest of the voyage to find room for their belongings. But Martha sent the cello off with Nikkos, instructing him to be careful with the precious instrument and to find a safe corner for it in the lounge. Next, Martha suggested they unpack all the reading material they had brought. They lined the books behind the rails on the shelves above their beds and stacked the magazines on the little coffee table in the sitting room: *Elle*, two *New Yorkers*, *Match*, *Vanity Fair*, *Oprah*, *The New York Review of Books*, *Vogue*, *Harpers*, and out of habit, two advertising journals, *Adweek* and *Shoot*. Their clothes could not possibly fit in the small closet so, after triage, some were left in the suitcases which were then slid underneath the bed. Lingerie and socks and pantyhose were folded carefully into two of the dresser drawers and in Martha's, underneath a black silk slip, she placed her .380 automatic. She had traveled alone too often to feel safe without it.

When they were finished making a home of the suite, Martha opened one of the cases of Scotch, found two glasses which barely fit behind the rails on the shelf above the sink, and toasted to casting off from the shore of complications.

"To us," Claudia added. She curled into one of the comfortable armchairs while Martha settled into the other. Martha felt the delicious transition into vacation indolence begin.

The first question about the circumstances of their fellow passengers came right after the first sip of Scotch had washed through Claudia with relaxing warmth. "So," she said abruptly, "why do you suppose Prince Jed al Hann's family didn't just fly home to Algeria? If they can charter a ship, they could certainly charter a plane."

Martha was pleased that she hadn't voiced this question first, though it had occurred to her. It was more fun to tease Claudia about her predictable curiosity than to guess at an answer.

"Claudia," she said, "you and Nikkos are going to be a problem, aren't you? My two sea sleuths. Let's get you a steward's uniform so you can move about the ship inconspicuously. We'll need to do something about your hair though, and you're way too tall, and your eyes aren't Mediterranean. Maybe colored contacts."

Claudia smiled and tugged off her heavy sweater. "I just think it's strange," she said. "If I wanted to travel in secrecy, I'd do it fast, at night, from private airport to private airport. I wouldn't leave in the middle of the day on a freighter."

Indeed, the conspicuousness of the prince's secret journey struck Martha as odd, but she didn't have Claudia's insatiable curiosity, and she didn't really care. Not right then, anyway. Not with Claudia sitting only feet way, her lovely long legs curled under her, her full breasts barely hidden behind her lacy bra, not with Claudia's exquisite, unaffected elegance taking her breath away and, as it had for years, washing across her in waves of desire.

"Come here," Martha commanded. And Claudia did.

CHAPTER 4

"They coming right now!"

An hour later Nikkos stood in the door that Martha held half open to guard their privacy. Behind her, Claudia sat on the floor, leaning against the chair where Martha had been sitting.

"Go on deck and look," the man went on excitedly. "Strange and strange. Two big black cars, just there, nobody getting out."

The women's cabin opened directly onto the exposed deck, just five feet from the ship's railing. Past Nikkos, Martha saw gray sky and rain and the tarred tops of warehouses. She found nothing appealing about the opportunity to look over the side of the ship, four stories down to the dock, for a glance at the party with whom they would be spending the next four weeks. Or, rather at the party with whom they would not be spending the next four weeks. She was about to thank Nikkos curtly for disturbing them and return to brushing Claudia's hair when Claudia came to the door, once again fully dressed.

"Nikkos," she said, "we'll be right there. Let me get my hat."

Martha looked at her lover's eyes. For years they had been dulled by the stress of deadlines and eight-hour flights and daily contamination with fashion's egomaniacs. Now those eyes again shone with a girl's brightness. Martha knew that before the Swan II had even left the dock, Claudia's spirit had begun to rejuvenate. She thanked Nikkos and closed the steel door.

"Claudia," she said, "wait for me."

Even though B deck was protected from above by A deck, the cold and rain blew in at them. Since staying dry was impossible, they decided they could get a better view from the main deck. Nikkos led the way through a labyrinth of companionways and heavy watertight doors and down steel stairwells until finally they were on the main deck, stepping over hoses and cables on their way to the rail.

"Look!" Nikkos pointed to two black Lincolns below them on the dock. The windows of both cars were tinted a smoky black. "They've been there for half hour, just parked. No doors open. Nothing moves."

A deep, muffled blast of the ship's horn made all three look up towards the funnel and then back down where there was nothing except the two big black cars sitting in the rain.

Martha plunged her hands deeper into the pockets of her wool overcoat, trying to get warmer, trying to feel less foolish, trying not to say what she was thinking, which was that this little excursion was a big waste of time. She looked over at Claudia who, with Nikkos, was leaning over the railing, as if effort would allow them to see inside the cars.

Martha was just about to announce that she was going back to the cabin when the front passenger door of the first car opened and a huge man in a dark suit got out. The man looked up; Martha could see his eyes focusing on them in pure hate. And then she noticed that his face was heavily pockmarked that that where his ears should be were what looked like little stubs. Even filtered through the rain and distance, the man's menacing presence was powerful. Martha jumped as he shook his fist at them angrily.

"We leave now," Nikkos said. He backed away from the railing and bumped into a winch bolted to the deck behind them. The seat of his soaking wet uniform was now covered in grease.

Claudia continued to stare down at the man, her curiosity finally rewarded. Martha, incapable of being intimidated for long, waved back to him. In response, the hideous man drew his hand across his throat as if slicing it open, and then got back into the car, slamming the door behind him. Martha imagined she felt the ship shudder.

A few snowflakes had begun to fall and it was becoming too cold to linger. Besides, Martha saw that Nikkos was panic stricken, as if the hideous man by the Lincoln had put a curse on him. "Please," he said, standing far enough from the rail that he could not be seen from below. "We must go now."

But just then, simultaneously, the front and back doors of both cars opened. Martha couldn't help but watch. The big man was first to get out. He glanced up towards Martha and Claudia at the railing, this time without the hostile recognition of their presence, and then nodded to someone inside the first car. The driver emerged. He was dressed in a thobe, a white, heavy robe, and a ghutra, a cloth headdress, which hung down between his shoulders in the shape of a V. He immediately glanced up to the railing, clearly having been informed of the women's presence there, and then leaned back into the car for two umbrellas. He handed one to the earless man.

The driver and the earless man opened the umbrellas. As if on cue, four women emerged, one from the first car and three from the second. They were all heavily veiled, each shrouded in a single, pleated drape that was formed at their heads into a kind of cap. From there the drape hung in volumes of silky black material to their ankles.

One of the women looked up to where Martha and Claudia stood. Her face was completely hidden behind a mesh of dark fabric but clearly she was looking at the two American women. Martha stared back fascinated. The woman was immediately ushered toward the two men by the other three women. Again, she looked up to the rail where Martha and Claudia watched but was quickly jerked forward by one of her companions. All were soon under the umbrellas, two black mushrooms moving steadily towards the ship. Martha and Claudia watched until the group was out of sight. Then the second Lincoln drove off, leaving the first still parked on the deck, its doors opened. There was nothing left to see.

"Martha, did you notice something strange about those people?"

Martha and Claudia were back in their cabin; the damp towels thrown on the floor made the suite look like a laundry room. They sat across from each other, their feet up on the single ottoman that served both chairs, Claudia in the flannel robe she had unpacked moments ago, and Martha wearing only a towel. Though they had been on board the Swan II for only two hours, and it was still not quite time to sail, Martha already felt a familiar affection for their little suite.

"No," she said, "nothing strange at all. Just a thug who threatened to kill us with his looks and four veiled women from another time and place being herded to our ship where they will be sequestered for weeks. No, nothing strange at all."

Claudia frowned. "Seriously, didn't you find something odd, something frightening about it all?"

"Oh," Martha said, "you mean frightening as in the thug whose face looks like it's made out of lava? The one with walnut shells where his ears should be? The one with the huge gun inside his coat, the gun he was conspicuously trying to hide? The one...?"

Claudia leaned forward and grabbed Martha's hand. "No. Stop, will you? I mean that woman, the one who looked up at us. She was being lead to the ship against her will, I'm sure of it."

Martha opened her mouth to dismiss this observation, along with Nikkos' ravings and their silly trip to the railing in the rain and even her willingness to act interested at all, but really, Claudia was right. The one veiled woman who had looked up at Martha and Claudia seemed to be asking for help, even pleading with the two women. And then Martha laughed to herself, suddenly understanding the imagination of sailors who for centuries had been seeing mermaids and sea monsters, turning the banal into the phantasmagoric. Only two hours on board and already she was already succumbing. But still...

Martha hated to admit it, especially given Claudia's flair for sensation and drama, but something about the scene on the dock had made her uneasy.

"Well," she said, "at least we don't have to worry about whatever was going on down there. What the prince's family does is none of our business."

Claudia looked steadily at her companion. "I wonder," she said, "if you're right."

CHAPTER 5

The Swan II had been out of port for an hour, moving through a sea that in spite of the gray, stormy day was pleasantly calm. Martha and Claudia had been invited to have cocktails at five o'clock with the captain and until then they sat in the armchairs and read, their feet occasionally play-fighting for the most comfortable spot on the ottoman.

From somewhere deep underneath them Claudia could feel the vibrations of the Swan II's steam turbines, and that, along with the short, rhythmic bowing of the ship into the waves, made her feel as if she was in the pouch of a gentle, purring animal.

Her amusing reverie was broken by a loud knock on the cabin door. "Miss Simmerhorn, Miss Bekele," a voice shouted, "it's Nikkos with towels you asked him to bring." Claudia got up, pulled the tie of her robe tight, and opened the door just enough to accept the towels. Nikkos had changed uniforms and his face had lost all its animation.

"Nikkos," Claudia said, "what's wrong?"

The man's reply was ready. "Captain say I'm nosy. Was very mad. Mystery people complain that we spy on them. Yell at captain, he yell at me."

Martha, sitting out of view of the cabin door, turned the page of the book she was reading by Wangari Muta Maathai. She heard the nervousness in Nikko's voice and smiled at the captain's good judgment; she hoped there would be no more playing at adventure. She tightened the towel wrapped over her breasts and returned her attention to Maathai's efforts to prevent the degradation of Kenya.

Claudia's voice, however, rang out across the savannah. "You tell the captain that you were helping us," she said firmly. "And tell the captain, no, we'll tell the captain that there was something wrong with that whole spectacle on the dock and that he should be concerned."

Martha left Africa in a hurry. "Claudia," she called, "please, give Nikkos our wet towels, take the fresh ones, and close the door. You're letting in the entire Atlantic."

Claudia turned to scoop the wet towels from around the cabin. Nikkos continued to speak through the partially open door. "No," he said, "I no longer talk to captain. This is long voyage, already."

When Nikkos had finally gone, Martha put her book aside, removed the towel, and started to dress for cocktails with the captain. She got as far as dropping her slip over her shoulders before deciding to let Claudia and Nikkos pursue their fantastic fascination with their fellow passengers without further comment, though certainly without further encouragement.

Martha turned from the dresser; Claudia stood as if waiting. Martha untied her lover's robe and ran her hands gently from Claudia's hips to her face. "It's time," she said, "that we meet this horrible captain."

The look in Claudia's eyes told Martha that she was sliding into arousal. Fervently she hoped that her loving ministrations would erase all thoughts of the mysterious passengers from Claudia's mind. At least for the moment.

CHAPTER 6

"Ms. Beneke, Ms. Simmerhorn, I am Captain Rappa. It is a pleasure to welcome you aboard the Swan II."

The captain was wearing a black uniform with gold braid around the cuffs and on the epaulets. Two medals were pinned to his breast pocket.

Martha nodded. "Thank you, captain. It is a pleasure to be here."

The captain removed his hat and placed it under his left arm. Then he extended the right hand and bowed. "You will find the ship and my crew in your service."

Except for an entire deck, Martha thought.

While Claudia charmingly engaged the captain in light, social pleasantries, Martha appraised the lounge. Along the sideboard that ran the length of one wall was a sink and built-in refrigerator, and above, shelves of liquor bottles and various crystal cocktail and wine glasses secured behind rails. On the other end of the sideboard was a built-in television /audio system, neither of which Martha knew they would use. Another wall was lined with bookshelves; volumes of old hardbacks stood behind glass doors, their slipcovers long lost or worn away. In the center of the room was a leather couch and, on either side, matching leather wingback chairs.

What Martha found most unexpected was the baby grand piano in the far corner of the room. She couldn't imagine anybody she had met so far being able to play. The captain's hands were too stubby, and Nikkos, well, she thought, unhappy with herself for being so critical, too simple. Anyway, Martha hoped for Claudia's sake that there was some member of the crew who could accompany her.

Overall, the room with its thick maroon carpet, lighting provided only by table lamps, and its dark, walnut-paneled walls, reminded

Martha of the Metropolitan Club in Manhattan, a place of private, hushed, and self-contained comfort. She was pleased.

At first, Claudia found Captain Rappa's formality a bit theatrical, even comic, but as they talked, she decided it wasn't a self-conscious, mimicked formality but the social uneasiness of a man used to being alone, looking forever towards the horizon. It was pleasantly clear that Captain Rappa was not going to be a social director; he was nothing other than a seventy-five year old sailor who cared only about the sea and his ship. After years of enduring the intimidated overtures of the fashion industry hangers-on and the strutting arrogance of the hip who always knew someone in Hollywood who could make something "fantastic" of her career, Claudia found the captain's indifference charming.

The captain invited Martha and Claudia to sit on the couch and went to the bar and filled three crystal glasses with champagne. "To all of us on the Atlantic," he said. He raised his glass to the women before nodding to the sea outside and then sank into one of the wingback chairs, relaxed but, the women noted, not entirely.

Martha glanced next to her at Claudia. Her legs were crossed at the ankles; one arm was stretched along the back of the couch, the other rested on her hip.

"Captain Rappa," Claudia said, "do please tell us about your medals." From many years of watching Claudia's battle with her imaginative curiosity, Martha knew this question was in an introduction to an interrogation of some sort.

"They are from many years ago but mean much to me," the captain replied. His hand automatically found the gold star hanging from a blue and red ribbon. "This was given to me by the Republic of South Viet Nam. I had a little vessel in a big typhoon off Ba Don, where we shouldn't have been. Saved some people who shouldn't have been there either. It was the biggest sea I've ever seen," he added.

Captain Rappa's fingers automatically found the other gold star, this one attached to a red and white ribbon. "And this," he said, "was given to me by the King of Denmark himself. They own Greenland, you know. Anyway, I like these two because they go well with my uniform." The captain chuckled. Claudia sensed he was amused by this innocent admission of vanity.

"What kind of cargo would they need on Greenland," she asked, "reindeer boots?"

Martha winced. The distinction between Claudia's humor and her cynicism was often indistinguishable.

"Reindeer boots?" the captain asked. Martha saw him turn to look out towards a horizon he couldn't see from the lounge. Clearly, he had not understood the joke. "No, the reindeer don't need boots. A tanker was in distress and we went a long way to find it." He looked back to Claudia and smiled. "Although taking boots to reindeer would probably have been more profitable."

"What kind of cargo do you have now?" Claudia asked.

"It's an open manifest," the captain explained. "A little bit of everything. Cobble plates and tractors and fertilizer and…"

Claudia interrupted. "Veiled women and their keepers?"

Martha watched as the captain's posture straightened; he was the master of an ocean-going vessel that had suddenly encountered something unrecognizable in its shipping lane. "They, like you, are passengers and guests," he said. "'Persons in Addition to Crew,' as we say."

Claudia leaned towards him. "But why all the secrecy? And the big man with the women. Who is he, I wonder? Don't you find the whole thing strange? Why not just fly home to Algeria? Certainly it would be faster."

Martha tried to catch Claudia's eye but her lover was focused on their host.

Captain Rappa's voice descended into a baritone, stiff and assertive. "Ms. Simmerhorn, the very privacy the company asked me to assure our fellow passengers is the very thing you are asking me to take away." He set his glass on the side table and reached for his cap, as if preparing to leave. Then, suddenly, he sat back and rubbed the side of his face as if testing to see if he had missed any spot shaving earlier. "Actually," he said, "perhaps we should talk a bit about the situation."

He looked directly at Martha, then Claudia. "I haven't even seen their passports," he said. "I know nothing about them. Do you know what a 'flag of convenience' is?"

Martha understood something about how loose maritime law was, but only as it related to getting refunds from cruise ship companies. She shook her head.

"It is a way to avoid registering a ship in certain countries in order to skirt certain regulations," Captain Rappa went on. "Insurance, crews' wages, ship safety, emigration can all be compromised this way. The safety of this ship, I assure you, has not been compromised, but this is the first time in my forty-three years at sea, all of them sailing under a flag of convenience, when I haven't really known the nature of my cargo. All protocol has been ignored."

Martha was startled at how quickly they had become the captain's confidantes. She hoped Claudia's inquiries would end here, but she sighed, disappointed, when she saw her lover curl her feet up under her and cross her arms over her breasts, a ball of intense curiosity.

"Do you really mean to say you know nothing else about these people?" Claudia demanded.

"Ms. Bekele, Ms. Simmerhorn," Captain Rappa said, as if reluctantly confessing, "I have made eleven trips to Viet Nam with munitions, have taken twenty tons of compressed air tanks marked 'biohazards' around Cape Horn in fifty-foot swells down to the Weddell Sea. I have had the Plimsol Line so far underneath the water with freight that only a diver could find it. And do you know what? This feels like the most dangerous cargo I have ever transported. So, please, do me a favor, leave the prince's family alone. It will be easy, I can assure you."

Martha looked at the expression on her companion's face. *Not for my beautiful Claudia, it won't*, she thought.

CHAPTER 7

By the time Martha and Claudia finished dinner, formally set and served to them in the lounge, it was ten o'clock. The wind and rain had increased and in the distance, on the port side, lightning punctuated the stormy blackness. They made their way down the interior companionway back to their cabin, avoiding the exposed deck passage. Already the labyrinth of watertight doors through bulkheads and steep, narrow stairwells was beginning to seem less complicated, almost familiar.

When the women got to their cabin, they found their beds turned down and an extra blue blanket folded at the foot of each one. A huge basket of fruit stood on their dresser. After the captain's gentle admonitions and the bottle of Merlot at dinner, Claudia's curiosity was reduced from active to passive, and now the comfort of their cabin— the big chairs, their familiar magazines and books, the double beds, the Swan II's rhythmic bowing into the sea—threatened to extinguish it altogether.

Claudia showered, put on a night gown, and then draped herself sideways across one of the big chairs, yards of pink satin falling across her legs and pooling beside her on the floor. She glanced at the condensation on the pipes that crossed the ceiling and then sat up a bit to watch Martha undress in the bedroom. Suddenly, she was swept by a nauseating uneasiness and swung around to look at the porthole directly behind her.

Not until the lightning flashed could she see the outline of an earless, pocked face. The belligerent man from the limousine. With more disgust than fear, she was up and at the door, but by the time it was open, the man had disappeared into the rainy night. It had all happened in a matter of seconds.

In the bedroom Martha was naked, massaging lotion into her legs when Claudia came in and grabbed her hands. Martha's delight disappeared immediately when she saw the look of alarm in Claudia's eyes.

"Martha, he was here, looking in through a porthole, the big ugly man from the car this afternoon."

Martha looked at Claudia with disbelief and then, suddenly understanding what had happened, rage. She tossed the bottle of lotion on the bed and drew Claudia to her.

But Claudia was more excited than afraid and broke away. "I told you so," she said. "I told you there was something wrong on this ship."

Martha hurried off to phone the captain, her anger at this assault to their privacy formidable. And while waiting for someone to answer her call she realized that any hope she had had of blunting Claudia's fascination with the mystery passengers was shattered. And this was part of what made her so angry. She wanted to spend her vacation with Claudia, not with Nancy Drew.

A mate finally answered.

"I want Captain Rappa, right now," Martha demanded.

Claudia listened to Martha's half of the conversation.

"You may get the captain," she said after a pause. "I assume that he is on the ship and that you can find him. Or must I?"

Claudia saw Martha's hand tighten around the receiver. "You are the problem right now," she replied to what was obviously the mate's question. "There has been a grave incident that requires immediate attention from the captain. I want you to understand this. Now I am going to hang up and you are going to send Captain Rappa to Ms. Bekele's suite."

The captain arrived ten minutes later, no longer in his dress uniform but wearing a blue sweater with the Swan II crest embroidered on it. Claudia told him what she had seen through the porthole.

"Ms. Simmerhorn," he replied, "I must admit I find it hard to believe that such a breach of safety could have occurred on my ship."

"Listen," Martha said angrily, "earlier this evening you as much as said you felt your ship was carrying a dangerous cargo. Well, now you know it is. And you had better do something about it."

Captain Rappa nodded. "I can assure you," he said, "that your privacy will not be violated again, even if it means I must place a guard outside your cabin. You will not be threatened by anything or anyone on my ship again." And without waiting for a reply from either woman, he left.

Even though they had moved the two twin beds together, Martha and Claudia slept in just one that night. It was Claudia's idea. She wasn't afraid, exactly. She wondered if she'd ever been afraid, really afraid, in her life. No, she decided, she hadn't. At least, not since Martha had come back into her life.

Claudia found Martha's hand in the dark and placed in on her thigh. And when Martha's strong and graceful hand slid Claudia's gown up, over her knees, to her thighs, Claudia forgot all about the big ugly man at the porthole, the woman being led onto the ship, and the guard outside their cabin. Alone in the dark with Martha, Claudia felt like the most loved and secure person in the world.

CHAPTER 8

The next morning the sky was clear but giant swells rocked the Swan II. At breakfast the little rails that ran along the edge of the tables had been raised in case the roll of the ship worsened. Martha was just about to cut into the cantaloupe when a mate knocked on the door to the lounge. Martha beckoned him inside. The mate handed her an envelope and departed. Inside was a short note from the captain.

"*The man at the window last night,*" she read silently, "*was Mr. Abbas Bindar. I spoke with him and he explained that he was unfamiliar with the ship, got lost, and was trying to find his way back to his cabin. He offers his apologies for startling you.*"

Martha handed the note to Claudia. She was satisfied with Captain Rappa's handling of the incident and returned to finish her breakfast with relish.

Claudia's reaction to the note was different. Once again she felt the purr of curiosity. If Mr. Abbas Bindar could find his way to their cabin, could Ms. Claudia Simmerhorn find her way to his?

After breakfast, the women discussed the need, if any, for ship-board routines. If they were so inclined, they could use the treadmill and free weights in the ship's tiny gym. Several hours each day could be spent writing in their journals. Years ago they had committed to keeping journals but had too often neglected the documents in favor of more social activities, like movies and the theatre.

Of course, they could read, another indulgence as their daily, work-a-day lives too often left them exhausted at the end of the day, ready only for bed.

Claudia had her cello, another love she had slowly, unconsciously abandoned for hours in international airports and alongside fashion runways.

Best of all, the women could spend lazy hours with each other. That was the greatest luxury—time to be alone together, to stand together at the portside rail, looking out at the giant rollers and the little explosions of sea spray, looking north, up towards perhaps Labrador or Greenland, to places where they were not known. A great luxury, to hold gloved hands, watch a raft of petrels, and feel their weight shift pleasantly shift with each roll of the sea.

The day passed, the sky remained clear and the rollers began to even out. At five o'clock they were in the lounge playing Scrabble when Nikkos came in with two crystal glasses and a bucket of ice on a silver tray. Martha hadn't seen him since their retreat from the rail the day before and was surprised that someone who had been as annoyingly and persistently pleasant as he had been yesterday had been so invisible today. With his head lowered, Nikkos placed the tray on the small table next to the women and backed away. When he was almost to the door he asked if there was anything else they needed.

Martha was trying to figure out how to get rid of her "j" and didn't look up from the game board.

"Nikkos," Claudia exclaimed, "what happened to your eyes?"

Martha's head shot up then and she saw that Nikkos' eyes were a dark purple and just about swollen closed.

"I fall," he replied curtly. "That's what happens sometimes on ships. Anything else, Miss Simmerhorn?"

"Nikkos," Martha said, further startled by his uncharacteristic tone, "have you seen the ship's doctor?"

"I fall last night, am fine now," he said. "Very busy. Ring if you need me." But instead of leaving the lounge, Nikkos stepped back into the room and walked over to the leather couch.

Martha watched as he punched and slapped the couch cushions back into shape, amused by what appeared to be a small tantrum. She looked at Claudia quizzically. Claudia, in response, just shrugged and rose to make them each a Scotch. Martha's "j" became part of "raj," crystal glasses pinged together in a toast, and Nikkos found another project in straightening the books on the shelves.

Martha's patience began to thin. "Nikkos," she said, her tone dismissingly polite, "are you sure you're all right?"

Nikkos kept his back to Martha and Claudia as he continued to work on the top shelf of books. Martha heard him mumble something, as if he were addressing the row of bindings, as if he didn't have the courtesy to address the women directly.

"Nikkos," Martha snapped, "if you expect to be heard you must talk to us, not to the wall. If you do not expect to be heard or have nothing to say, please leave us alone."

Slowly, Nikkos turned; the look on his face was pathetic. What little of his eyes could be seen looked scared and confused. "I am sorry. I don't know what to do. I will go now."

Claudia looked at the little man with concern. "Nikkos," she said, "did someone do that to you? Did someone hit you?"

Martha groaned; here was another interruption of their tranquility. "Try to remember," she whispered to Claudia. "He's supposed to take care of us. We're not supposed to take care of him."

But it was too late. Nikkos stepped away from the bookshelves, eager to tell his story. "The big man hit me last night," Nikkos said. "I was by his cabin and he say 'You spying' and I say 'No,' and then he says he wants all my keys so I can't spy more and I say 'No' and he hits me and takes them anyway. He has no ears and he scares me."

Martha, ever the corporate executive, calmly triaged the crises. She identified three. First, after this latest incident Claudia was going to be insatiably curious no matter what Martha said or did to stop her. Second, Nikkos was annoying but pathetic and clearly in need of some sort of help. Third, and this was the realization that she was most reluctant to make, if Mr. Bindar had Nikkos' keys, then perhaps it was no accident that he was outside their cabin the night before. And if he still had Nikkos' keys, then maybe that night he would be inside their cabin. It was clear what crisis to tackle first.

"Nikkos, what time did this happen?" Martha asked in a tone that offered Nikkos no encouragement to embellish or complain.

"At dinner time."

Claudia got up, put her hands into the deep pockets of her sweater and walked over to the bar. She knew how curt Martha could be when she wanted only essential information, not useless chat, and was embarrassed for Nikkos. But she was also eager to hear every word.

"Have you told the captain that you don't have your keys?" Martha went on.

"No. Not at first. Then I do so this morning and he get them back. He…"

"Nikkos. Were you spying?"

Claudia choked on her Scotch at the tactlessness of Martha's question.

"No. I don't…"

"So, what were you doing on A deck last night?" she demanded. "We were told the prince's family have their own staff."

"I go there to see if I can help."

"Weren't you told by the captain not to bother those passengers?"

Nikkos looked at his shoes. "Yes," he said. "Big mistake going there." And then, mumbling again, he added, "Big mistake signing on this trip."

"Nikkos." There was no trace of sympathy left in Martha's voice; it was flat and cold. "We need to leave the prince's family alone. That shouldn't be too hard now, should it?"

"No, Miss Bekele. I…"

"Thank you and I hope you feel better in the morning."

Nikkos walked to the door but stopped before leaving. "Miss Bekele, Miss Simmerhorn, don't tell the captain I tell you about the keys. Please. He made me promise not to tell but I thought you should know."

"You didn't have to be quite so rude to him," Claudia said when the door had closed behind the little man. "He can't help being pathetic."

Martha tried not to be annoyed by Claudia's angry outburst, but she was. "I am not on this trip to worry about a trouble making steward," she said. "If he can't be unobtrusive then Captain Rappa needs to find us another steward."

Just barely did Martha stop herself from revealing what she was really thinking, that there might after all be something very bad on board the Swan II. And that there might also be something very bad about Nikkos.

CHAPTER 9

Martha looked forward to having dinner with the captain. Claudia had volunteered to play the cello afterwards. But first, over bottles of the ship's best wines, Martha planned to conduct a polite inquisition. She was a conspirator in the investigation now, but unlike Claudia, who was romantically curious about the prince's family, Martha only wanted reassurance about their own safety and confirmation of Captain Rappa's trustworthiness.

Martha opened the top dresser drawer. Before selecting a pair of panties she checked to make sure her Beretta was still there. Seeing the little gun made her feel far less at the mercy of the big ugly man on A deck.

Claudia's long silky hair hung down the back of her floor length, deep purple velvet dress. Martha wore a silver sequined, ankle-length sheath. The dress made her feel like an unapproachable African enchantress. Together the women walked to the lounge to wait for the arrival of Captain Rappa and his first mate.

They didn't have to wait long. At exactly seven o'clock, Captain Rappa arrived with the first mate, a young Lebanese with a last name so phonetically wonderful that, when invited to call him simply Ben, Martha was relieved.

The conversation over the first course was mostly about ships and the sea, a subject that allowed the two men to move away somewhat from their self-conscious awkwardness. They talked about Flinder's bars and chronometers and longitude and Loran systems and storms.

Martha and Claudia learned that the little rails that ran around the tables were called "fiddles." The Captain told them about using fire hoses to repel pirates in the China Sea and about being off shore in the Sudan during a cholera quarantine with a cargo of 200,000 chickens. It was fun, but all the while Martha waited for an opportunity to change the subject to the one that really mattered.

Finally, the main course was served. "Ben," Martha asked mildly, when she'd neatly cut into the crust of the beef Wellington, "what happened to Nikkos? The poor man looks awful." She watched the first mate look uneasily at the captain for the answer.

"He fell last night," the captain said mechanically, "in the companionway below. Nikkos sometimes is too busy to be careful."

Martha glanced at Claudia; Claudia winked, clearly pleased that Martha now shared her open curiosity.

"He looked so sad this afternoon," Claudia said, "and he's such a sweet man. What else does he do on board, not just help us I hope?"

"Nikkos cleans officers' rooms, too," Ben replied, "and helps in the kitchen, sometimes the laundry, wherever we need him. Sometimes he just disappears. But first, he is to take care of passengers."

"All the passengers?" Claudia asked.

"Not on this voyage," the captain replied stiffly. "The prince's family has its own staff. Nikkos has nothing to do with them. I was under the impression you knew that."

"Yes," Martha said. "We'd forgotten." She speared another piece of the beef Wellington. There was no more pretense at banter or light dinner conversation. Martha's eyes on the Captain were laser hot. "Captain," she asked, "are all the bulkhead doors locked?"

Captain Rappa and Ben answered simultaneously.

"No."

"Yes."

"Well," Martha asked, "which is it?"

Martha watched as Ben pondered the wine in his glass, as if were suddenly fascinated by its clarity, by the way it looked while delicately twirled in his glass, by the way it left a bit of a viscous film on the side.

The captain looked at Martha with strained patience and steered into the storm. "Ms. Bekele," he said, "is there something bothering you?"

Martha shrugged. "I am simply wondering how Mr. Bindar could have gotten to our cabin if all the bulkhead doors are locked. And if they aren't locked, I'm wondering what is to stop him from getting to our cabin again. Finally, I think it curious that the same night Mr. Bindar found his way to our cabin, Nikkos slipped in the companion-way and suffered such a nasty injury. It was quite a night, wasn't it?"

The first mate looked seasick, and now Claudia was twirling the wine in her glass.

"I don't know how Mr. Bindar found his way to your cabin," the captain replied after a tense moment. "The bulkhead doors which would allow access between his cabins and yours are locked. Someone must have forgotten to lock them last night, but I can assure you that they are locked now. Mr. Bindar will not be bothering you again. Nor, I hope, will you be bothering him."

"And Nikkos' black eyes?"

"He fell."

Martha noticed that although his tone hadn't changed, the captain's body language had. Now he leaned forward, his elbows on the table, his posture almost aggressive.

Martha was about to explain to the captain the physiology of black eyes, how unlikely it would be that simply falling, no matter how one hit one's head, would produce the kind of trauma that Nikkos had sustained, but the radio on the captain's belt beeped and he excused himself, looking immensely relieved.

While waiting for him to return, Martha reviewed what she had learned. First, that Mr. Bindar could not have gotten to their cabin without taking Nikkos' keys and probably had taken them for that very purpose. Second, that the captain was very capable of lying to them.

She was deciding what to do next when Captain Rappa returned with a request that made pursuing the subject, for the time being, less urgent. "Mr. Bindar," he said, "has asked if two members of his party could attend Ms. Simmerhorn's cello recital after dinner."

Martha looked at Claudia, stunned by this request.

"How did Mr. Bindar know I was going to play?" Claudia asked.

The captain paused for a moment before replying. "Honestly," he said, "I don't really know."

CHAPTER 10

The cello was foreplay, meant for an audience of one. It was really only for Martha that Claudia played; her music began a night of rapture that could only end with the two women in bed, their legs wrapped around each other, Martha's wonderfully strong hands moving underneath the silk of Claudia's nightgown. Without Martha, weeks and even months could go by without Claudia's touching the instrument. An expectant audience in a philharmonic hall could not change that.

Martha's special request could. She had asked Claudia to play for the captain and first mate as a gesture of civility. Claudia had reluctantly agreed, not at all excited about the prospect. Until, that was, the addition of the two unexpected listeners. Now, Claudia was brimming with anticipation. Finally, something tangible was about happen; they were about to meet two of the prince's family. Her curiosity about the mystery passengers might just be assuaged. Maybe, just maybe, she would learn answers to some of the questions that had been gathering stormily in her mind.

And so by the end of dinner the conversation had again become relaxed. Claudia didn't even bother to ask about the number of doors, if any, that needed to be unlocked for their guests to gain access to the lounge. She would save that question for later, or perhaps, never even need to ask it.

After dinner the table was cleared and the room converted back to the sea-going lounge it was meant to be. Martha retreated to one of the wingback chairs with a glass of Merlot and unfolded into it as if it were a huge, gentle hand. Her eyes were already softening with the anticipation of pleasure.

Claudia watched the captain anxiously approach Martha, as if sensing that he had to reach her before she completely withdrew from the world.

"Ms. Bekele," she heard the captain say. "May I ask that in deference to our Muslim guests you finish your wine before they arrive? I would like to make them feel as reasonably comfortable as we can."

Claudia knew what Martha's response would be.

"You're being silly, Captain Rappa," Martha said pleasantly. "They are our guests, not we theirs. If they find the wine or the music too offensive there's an entire deck to which they can flee." And then she looked away, dismissing with a smile any possibility of further discussion with the captain.

Captain Rappa bowed and took his seat next to the first mate in one of the straight-back chairs placed behind Martha, as far away as possible from the leather couch they left reserved for the guests.

Claudia carefully removed the cello from its gray, fiberglass case. Then she sat and cradled it between her velvet-covered thighs. A long, deep blast from the Swan II, warning the empty night of its presence, interrupted her preparations. She laughed.

"My first piece," she said, "will be Vivaldi's A# concerto for cello and fog horn."

Claudia leaned over the dark, rich cherry wood and lifted the train of her hair, which shone like the cello's luster, over her right shoulder. She began then to tune the instrument by making small adjustments to its pegs.

Martha observed her lover. Claudia seemed to have entered a dimension of concentration inaccessible to those watching her. Martha knew the joy that was coming and began even then to warm with adoration and arousal. Nor was the intensity of the moment entirely lost on the captain and the first mate. Even before Claudia had begun to play, the reverence of Chartres filled the room.

The spell was temporarily broken by the appearance of the two guests. They seemed to glide in to the lounge, their perfume and the jingle of jewelry announcing their entry like a barely audible fanfare. The two women were sheathed entirely in black, but instead of the shroud of formless, heavy material they had been wearing when they boarded the ship, their black abaayas were made of sheer, exquisite Italian silk, the hems and sleeves embroidered in gold. Veils covered the women's faces but the material was thin, and when they moved just right, Claudia caught a glimpse of large dark eyes.

The women crossed the room to the couch. One wore red slippers and when she sat, her abaaya gathered a bit underneath her, exposing graceful ankles that she crossed before looking down to the floor.

The other woman sat next to her. She allowed herself to look around the room before fixing her eyes on Claudia. Then she leaned into her companion and whispered something that made them both laugh. Now both women stared blatantly at Claudia, as if they thought they couldn't be seen, as if their veils rendered them invisible.

Captain Rappa rose and approached the women in welcome. But his formal greeting in English was not understood or it was ignored because neither woman made any response. From the wingback chair, Martha attempted an introduction in French but there was still no response, only stares from behind the veils. Martha wondered if the two women were struck dumb by the small, social expectation of being pleasant, or if they were just plain rude.

Claudia was fascinated. She remembered stories she'd heard while working at W2, stories about wealthy Saudi men in London closing Harrod's for an afternoon so that their women could shop in privacy. She had heard other, more disturbing stories, too, about female circumcision and ritual baths and odas, and now these dark shapes on the couch and the glimpse of dark eyes fueled her reckless romanticism. She smiled kindly at the women but could not tell if they were smiling back.

Claudia looked then to Martha, who shrugged with amusement at the awkwardness of their little shipboard society. And then Martha's eyes directed her to look over her shoulder at the open door. Mr. Bindar stood just outside, in the sea night, looking in.

Claudia resisted a shudder of uneasiness, tapped her bow against the instrument, and began.

Martha felt the Schumann Cello Concerto cover her in ways a veil or a sea never could, saw Claudia's eyes soften and shine the way they did when she made love to her, and then Martha became the cello cradled in the velvet-covered legs, each movement of the bow Claudia's hands on the secret, wonderful places of her body.

When Claudia stopped playing, Martha had no idea what had become of their guests.

CHAPTER 11

Several uneventful days passed. Martha and Claudia read, wrote in their journals, played the board games they found in the lounge. On calm days they placed lounge chairs on the deck and lay wrapped in blankets, reading, dozing, watching the sea and sky. Once they watched the ocean from the bridge, then went below deck and saw the engine room from steel catwalks high above, watched as the first mate traced their course on a chart. Another time they climbed into and then out of a lifeboat and decided it was much nicer to just do nothing. Around three o'clock each day they retreated to their suite for a short nap.

Nikkos came and went in his obsequious way, Mr. Bindar and the veiled women remained in seclusion but hardly forgotten.

One morning the sea was particularly heavy. The Swan II rolled and pitched and at breakfast the fiddles were up. Nikkos struggled through the door with a huge tray and placed in on the edge of the table. Martha noted that his eyes, though still black, were much less swollen. Even more striking was his renewed joviality.

"Miss Beleke, Miss Simmerhorn, two pretty ladies on ugly day. I make the cappuccinos myself. No one make them better than Nikkos." He put the cups in front of the women, making sure the little symbols on the saucers were squared directly in front of them. "You feel okay? No seasick?"

"We feel fine and you look much better," Claudia said, as Nikkos served the rolls and cantaloupe. "Nikkos, do you know who invited our guests to hear me play in the salon the other night?"

"No, I ask engineer. He not tell me much."

"But Nikkos," Martha asked pleasantly, hoping that Nikkos would indict himself and save her the work, "somehow the prince's family knew Claudia was going to play."

Nikkos shrugged. "Probably the captain tell," he said. "He and Mr. Bindar good friends. They smoke cigars on the bridge. Laughing and serious together all the time."

Martha exchanged an incredulous glance with Claudia and waited for Nikkos to cut squares of a frittata and serve them. "Nikkos," she asked then, "are you sure you didn't tell Mr. Bindar or anyone in his party about Claudia playing the cello after dinner?"

Nikkos shook his head vehemtnly. "I don't talk to any of them since I get hit."

Martha believed him. She assumed she was witnessing one of the little man's rare moments of honesty.

"You think Nikkos crazy Greek?" he laughed. "That Bindar man like Minotaur. If you find him, trouble. So why find him? I go make your rooms now. Bring you another coffee when you're ready. Just ring."

That the captain and Mr. Bindar were friendly was a troubling revelation to Martha. Although it didn't mean that their safety was jeopardized, it did mean that Captain Rappa was indeed a liar and that she and Claudia were somewhere in the Mid-Atlantic among company they couldn't trust. Isolation was what they had wanted, but perhaps not quite in this way. Martha was wondering about the degree of civility she would use the next time she saw the captain when she was suddenly heartened by the knowledge that back in their cabin, in the top dresser drawer, lay her little silver gun.

Since her brief concert, Claudia had been wondering why only two of the four women they had seen boarding the ship had been allowed to hear her play. She just knew that one of the women who didn't attend was the one who had been forced onto the ship. And now that the entire ship, except for Nikkos, seemed to be conspirators, Claudia was no longer willing to be excluded from the intrigue. She absolutely would find out what was going on.

She remembered an article on design piracy she had edited for W2 several years earlier, and how impressed she had been with the writer's courageous investigation of the Hong Kong garment markets. By that time, Claudia was growing bored with writing articles about nothing more substantial than the wardrobes of the wealthy. Maybe, Claudia thought now, faced with a troubling mystery of unknown proportions—was a kidnapping afoot?—maybe now was the time she should try her hand at writing something truly important. Maybe here was a story that would launch her career as freelance journalist.

Most of the day the Swan II rode from trough to crest, bowing and rising through huge seas. Sometimes the entire bow disappeared straight down, into the spray; sometimes it rose up so straight it seemed to be looking into the sky for help. But there was no help from that direction. The rain fell steadily, an upside down ocean.

Inside the lounge magazines and books slid back and forth across the table, and glasses and bottles rattled behind the bar. The ship groaned as if its metal plates were being jammed together and then pulled apart. It was easy for Claudia to understand why sailors developed such affection for their ships and for their ships' ability to remain buoyant in monster seas.

There was nothing much else to do but wait out the storm. Reading made Claudia queasy, and even standing was a bit of a problem. Claudia and Martha attempted to play cribbage, but most of their attention, both fascinated and frightened, remained on the storm outside.

Several hours after breakfast, Ben, the Lebanese first mate, came in. He was wearing a yellow, oilskin raincoat that made him look like a giant school-crossing guard. He assured them that this was a "fun little squall" and that a calmer sea was just a few hours away. Then he handed Claudia a package about the size of a small shoebox and told her that he had been instructed to deliver it to her. Ben left, leaving puddles of seawater behind.

The package was wrapped in an Arabic newspaper. Claudia admired the columns of lovely squiggles and arcs and half-moons, then carefully removed the paper. The box was made of stiff tope leather. The lid was hinged so that it opened like a chest, and inside, on top, was a card, written in French, in a beautiful, elaborate hand.

"Miss Claudia Rhodes,
Your music was lovely.
You are music."

The card was not signed. A purple silk-velvet scarf was wrapped around something heavy, and as Claudia unrolled it she was reminded of a child's nesting doll. Finally, she turned the last fold and, in stunned disbelief, stared. Diamonds, forty of them, probably one-carat stones, were set in the links of a heavy gold chain. Against the dark silk/velvet scarf the piece shone like a miniature Milky Way.

"Are they real?" Martha's voice was hushed.

Claudia nodded and lifted the piece out of the box, matched its length against her wrist and realized it was meant for the ankle. And then she noticed something else and she felt a wave of foreboding. The ends of the anklet were not meant to be clasped together. They were meant to be locked.

The piece wasn't an anklet at all, it was a shackle, a bejeweled fetter that once joined, could only be opened with a miniature key. Claudia checked the box. There was no key.

Claudia looked steadily at Martha. For a minute neither woman spoke. The fetter lay on the table between them like a deadly asp.

Finally, in a desperate attempt to prevent revulsion from turning completely into terror, Claudia gestured gracefully toward the box. "This year's Tiffany line of restraints," she said, "features a spectacular piece with no fewer than forty diamonds on an unbreakable gold chain. Best, its sturdy lock will make her yours forever."

Martha didn't laugh. "This isn't just tasteless," she said, "it's obscene. Those women, the prince's family. Only they could afford such vulgar opulence. But how could any woman think this is funny or cute?"

Claudia saw fear in her companion's eyes, eyes that had always been bright with confidence. She felt slightly sick.

"Something is very, very wrong," Martha said, almost as if speaking to herself. It made Claudia wonder: were they being watched, spied on, even now?

"That woman," Claudia said softly. "I'm more certain than ever that she was taken on board the ship against her will."

Martha tried to stand but the roll of the ship made her collapse inelegantly back into her seat. "I've had enough," she said. "The captain is a liar. He will explain to us his numerous lapses in honesty, one by one." Martha pointed to the leather box. "And then," she added, "he and his apparent friend Mr. Bindar can explain to us the meaning of this horrible thing, this threat, before taking it back."

Claudia nodded, as if agreeing, but she had already planned her own course of action. She would visit the veiled women and she would try to read the dark eyes behind the veils, try to find the captive one, try to save her. She knew that Martha would disapprove and so first she had to figure out when and how to sneak away from her companion.

And then, how to steal Nikkos' keys.

CHAPTER 12

By the afternoon the sea had calmed and little shafts of sunlight shone through the circle of gray horizon. But as the storm subsided, Martha's sense of foreboding increased. She needed a drink to quell her mounting anxiety and suggested an early cocktail hour.

The women went back to their cabin to dress for dinner. It was a custom they had adopted almost from their reunion ten years earlier, a delicious ritual preserved from a long gone society. Being glamorous was a small, personal gift they could give each other, but a meaningful one.

Claudia took a shower, dried, and with a huge bath towel wrapped around her, sat on the floor at Martha's feet for her hair to be combed. The strokes, at first tentative and gentle as they sought kinks and snarls, became longer and more sure as the comb met less and less resistance and as her hair began to glow. Claudia could feel the ship roll beneath her, could feel the rhythmic strokes of the comb through her hair, could feel the million tiny vibrations of its teeth massage her scalp. She dropped the towel and looked over her shoulder at Martha, asking permission.

Martha took Claudia gently by her shoulders and guided her all the way around until the two women were facing each other. Slowly, with deliberation, Claudia slid Martha's slip up and then, finding the lace edge of Martha's panties, curled them down and off. Her hands still on Claudia's shoulders, Martha pulled her in, and then locked Claudia's head in the warm vice of her thighs.

Martha felt Claudia's damp hair against her skin, felt Claudia's hands now on top of her legs, her nails softly scratching, softly digging. And when Claudia was at just the right spot, Martha's legs tightened. Claudia's grip became firmer as her tongue flicked and licked just as

ACROSS

Martha liked it, just as she wanted it. Faster and faster, moans and deep, gasping breaths, it went on until the finale of an orgasm that washed through Martha in convulsive waves of utter rapture.

And for a moment the horrible fetter was forgotten.

CHAPTER 13

Claudia's chance to pry information from Nikkos came forty-five minutes later. While Martha was bathing, Claudia went ahead to the lounge where Nikkos was preparing for cocktail hour, assembling ice and cheese and "little bites".

Nikkos was chatty. He complained about the rough sea, the nasty weather, the rust underneath his berth, the chicken bone he found in his soup at lunch. And no, he informed Claudia before she could ask, he hadn't seen Mr. Bindar or his party, and as far as he was concerned they had fallen off the ship into the sea and he hoped they had been eaten by sharks.

Using the momentum of Nikkos' babble, Claudia slipped in a question. "Nikkos," she said, "if someone didn't have keys, could they get from A deck to B deck some other way?"

Nikkos continued to cut the Jarlsburg into perfect wedges and to fan the crackers around the border of a silver tray. "Easy, Miss Simmerhorn," he said. "Just go through kitchen, stairs go right up. Other ways, too, but that is easiest." And then he halted his preparations and looked up at Claudia. "You ask questions that make me nervous. I don't want to talk about them. You leave those people alone, I leave them alone. You like me to cut up apple, too?"

Yes, Claudia thought, cut an apple, make a mess. I'll clean up and take the things back to the kitchen.

As Martha reached behind her for the zipper to her dress, she decided to excuse herself after drinks and, alone, find Captain Rappa.

And she would be prepared for whatever might come of that meeting. Martha opened her dresser drawer, retrieved the silver pistol and slipped it into her evening bag.

Though the ship was steady enough for Scrabble neither woman felt much like playing. Instead, they engaged in a slightly strained conversation that drifted from Willa Cather to Gordon Parks to the director of the Metropolitan Museum of Art to the small hole Martha had found in the hem of her cashmere skirt. To everything but what both women were really thinking about.

Claudia watched the crackers disappear, watched the wedges of Jarlsburg erode away to the rind. When Nikkos came to remove the remains of their 'little bites', she dismissed him. Nikkos eyed the empty tray, shrugged, and left the lounge.

Soon after, Martha excused herself to take a bit of a rest before dinner. Claudia assured her of an uninterrupted forty minutes. As soon as Martha left for the cabin, Claudia grabbed the silver tray and slipped out of the lounge.

The kitchen was easy to find; she had watched Nikkos carrying trays in its direction for days. Claudia walked along the narrow deck between rail and superstructure towards the stern. She tried several doors, found one that opened into the smell of curry and was there.

The kitchen staff was Filipino. Claudia smiled and placed the tray on a counter. The staff smiled back awkwardly, uncertain, it seemed, what protocol should be when a passenger was in their kitchen. Claudia immediately spotted a door next to a long, stainless steel sink, and, using the arrogant ramp walk that she despised but imitated perfectly, walked past the staff and over the high sill of the door.

Like all the other stairs on board the ship, the ones facing Claudia were narrow and steep, almost more of a ladder. Excited to be close to the forbidden deck, but worried that someone from the kitchen would come after her, Claudia practically ran up the steel stairs. At the top she found another watertight door. She pushed down on the giant lever and opened the door slowly, even though she knew that anyone on the other side would certainly hear the heavy latches clank open.

Claudia stepped in to a small, gray room, another in the ship's maze of similar rooms, which made finding one's way so disorienting. This room was empty except for a steel table, two chairs, and a counter with hot plates and a sink. Claudia guessed it was the serving station for the dining room. There was nothing in it now except for a tea kettle on a burner over a small blue flame and a tall brass tea maker. In one wall of the room was a double-hung wooden door, doubtless leading into the dining room. In another wall was another watertight door, opening, Claudia was sure, onto A deck.

She opened this door, ducked through, and found herself on an outside passageway identical to the one on the deck below. In the wet dusk she felt utterly alone, as if she were on a windswept, desolate, eternally crepuscular planet of exploding spindrift. The wind whistled through cables all around and somewhere a door or hatch banged maniacally again and again. Claudia was dressed for dinner, not for standing in the wet cold, shivering, without any idea which way to go. She felt foolish and scared, but she was determined to find something important before she went back to join Martha for dinner.

Quietly, Claudia went along the rail forward. She tried to peek into the portholes as she went, but each one was covered from the inside. She did not want to risk going onto the open deck at the bow, so when she got to the last cabin, she turned and walked back towards the stern. The first porthole she came to there, too, was covered.

She was getting too cold and wet now to waste her time looking into more covered portholes. With no other thought but to relieve the frustration of unrequited adventure before she got back to Martha and warmth, she tried opening a door.

At first, it didn't budge. Then Claudia saw that a key had been left in the lock, perhaps meant not for keeping someone from getting in, but for keeping someone from getting out.

Boldly, she turned the large brass key, pushed open the door, and was suddenly engulfed by terror.

On the floor of the room was spread a large Persian rug; carpeted pillows had been placed around the border. And in the middle of the rug was a woman. Her hands were tied behind her back and her ankles and knees were bound.

The woman twisted her head and shoulders to look at Claudia. Claudia felt faint. The woman, probably in her late twenties, was gagged with a device that looked like a horse's bridle. She wore a plain, sleeveless dress that was cinched around her knees by the ropes that bound her. She looked at Claudia now with dark, pleading eyes, eyes filled with both anger and humiliation, and then shook her head, as if trying to shake the bridle loose.

Claudia stood absolutely still as the bound woman rolled completely over toward her. She watched as the woman's whole body tensed and went rigid against the ropes, as if straining to break free. Then, the woman sank back into submission. She moaned and was still, only her eyes locked directly onto Claudia, still animated with pleading.

The quality of Claudia's horror registered at first as disbelief. There was no young woman bound on the rug in front of her. Claudia wasn't somewhere on the vast Atlantic, trapped on a ship with people who could have done such a thing to a fellow human being. She remembered sitting on the floor between Martha's legs, her hair being combed. She wanted Martha. She wanted this poor young woman and her awful companions and even the ship to just go away. She wanted to be playing Dvorak's Cello Concerto as she had long ago at her uncle's estate on Deer Island in Maine.

But there, undeniably, were this woman's pleading eyes, her contorted body, her dark hair caught behind her neck by the wide leather strap of the bridle. Disbelief became the urge to action. Claudia would not leave this woman behind.

Terrified and outraged, she darted into the cabin and over to the bound woman. Just as her hands found the buckle behind the woman's head, a coarse voice behind her ordered, "Leave her!"

He was on her immediately, jerking Claudia to her feet and dragging her to the door. Then he threw her roughly onto the deck.

"Now you see what you want?" he demanded. Mr. Bindar stood over her, his bald, earless head like a Halloween mask, his hyena eyes sunken in skin that looked like layers of desiccated, yellowing latex. "Now you know what trouble is."

Claudia curled away from this monster. She was soaking wet and the sleeve of her dress had been ripped off. She tried to get to her feet but slipped on the wet deck and fell. She heard the hiss of spray and the wind hum in cables and thought for a moment of cello strings; she felt the pulmonary throb of the engine decks beneath her; and she watched water wash across the deck and out the scupper by her head. She waited. Right above her a lifeboat swung from squeaky davits, "Capacity 65" painted on its side. Claudia slowly looked to one side and then the other.

Mr. Bindar was gone.

CHAPTER 14

"Is this your ship, Captain Rappa?"

Martha didn't want there to be any seam through which resolution to the problem could escape. She wore a black wool dress and a single strand of pearls. What was on the one hand unadorned elegance was, on the other hand, almost martial.

Two hours had passed since Claudia had come bursting into the lounge, drenched, both knees bleeding, her eyes desperate. Martha, who had been sitting on the couch worried about her missing companion, had just been about to go to the captain with her concern. The tale of Claudia's misadventure—the brutal attack on her person!—reinforced Martha's feeling that they were very much in danger on a very sick ship.

She had taken Claudia back to their cabin, given her a bath and a Scotch, and only then, after having heard the whole story and feeling assured that Claudia was in no need of a doctor, had she summoned the captain to the lounge.

Martha's angry, demanding tone made the captain look to Claudia as if for help. Claudia was seated in one of the big wingback chairs, a blanket wrapped around her shoulders. She looked small, exhausted, as if a fire had gone out of her. Even more than Martha's tone, Claudia's despair seemed to unnerve the captain. He looked back to Martha and replied, "I am, as you know, in command."

Martha didn't bother to hide the disdain she felt so strongly. "Do you have any idea what is happening, captain, on your vessel?"

"I know everything about the Swan II," Captain Rappa shot back, "more than you can imagine, even the names of the rats. And if you would leave the Swan II to me, this trip would be more pleasant for all of us."

"Even for that woman tied up in her cabin on the deck above?"

The captain's shoulders visibly tensed.

"How Ms. Simmerhorn got access to her I don't know. Mr. Bindar is here to protect the privacy of the prince's family. You were told to leave them alone and you didn't. I am now forced to put a guard on your deck to make sure you do. This is a matter of a foreign government, their internal, legitimate business. I didn't realize at first what the prince's family was doing on my ship, but I knew they had State Department clearance to be here, and the steamship company and I guaranteed them the privacy that their papers of transport stipulated."

Martha opened her mouth but the captain went on, more loudly.

"Now, I don't like what is happening, either, but it is not my place to become involved. And it is not your place, either. You are not at home anymore, Ms. Bekele, where there is some guarantee of decency. You are on the way to Algeria, probably the most dangerous country in the world. It has been at war with others and itself for over fifty years. The country is rife with terrorists, Islamic fundamentalists, corrupt government agents, revolutionaries, police, death squads, gangs, criminals in palaces and on camels. And somewhere in this mess we have taken sides and in the name of diplomacy allowed what you should never have seen. This is not DisneyWorld, Ms. Bekele, and you are to leave it alone."

The captain turned toward the door, but Martha stepped around him. Her fury would not allow him to leave just yet.

"This is not about Algerian politics and you know it," she spat. "I want you to get Ms. Simmerhorn, that poor captive woman, and me off this ship. You can play all the international games you want after we leave. Both Ms. Simmerhorn and Nikkos have been assaulted by your cigar-smoking companion and you have a young woman on board restrained beyond any reasonable measure of need. God knows what her offense is, dancing? Seeing herself in the mirror without her veil on? Now, you either arrange to have all of us transferred to another ship or drop us off at the nearest port. If you don't, you are holding us on your ship against our will. That's called kidnapping. And you are participating in the treatment of a young woman that must be a violation of any human rights standards. I promise I will see you punished if either continues."

But Martha's furious words had no visible effect on Captain Rappa. "The young woman will be getting off in Algeria in four days," he said, "and you will be getting off in Turkey two days after that. As originally planned. Good night."

The captain's hand was on the door lever when Martha grabbed his arm and pulled him around. Though she felt the first panic of helplessness, her eyes still burned with fury and she did not let go of the captain's arm.

"I will use your ship-to-shore radio, now," she said. "Show me where it is. And don't ever turn your back on me."

The captain removed Martha's hand from his arm and pushed it away. "You may phone your embassy in Algeria, as soon as they reestablish one, although it may be a few years yet."

For the first time in her adult life, Martha could think of nothing to say.

Now that the confrontation was about to end, the captain's expression and tone became almost conciliatory. "I am sorry, Ms. Bekele, but until you get off the ship in Turkey, we are incommunicado. If you plan to send an email, don't bother. We will jam all signals. But once again, I can assure that you and Ms. Simmerhorn will be safe until we reach Turkey. And now I must assure my other passengers that they will be safe from you."

Martha continued to stare at the door for several minutes after the captain had left. She felt rooted to the spot, caught in the vice of disbelief.

This can't be happening, she thought. *There must be something I've missed, another option, something I can do to save us all.*

Finally, Martha turned. She walked over to where Claudia sat in one of the comfortable chairs, perched on the arm, and almost absent mindedly stroked Claudia's hair.

Claudia looked up. In her eyes was a plea for reassurance. But Martha had none to give. She looked away from Claudia and stared off at some distant, safe shore that they seemed forever doomed to pass.

CHAPTER 15

Two days passed without incident. Except for the new presence of a mate outside their cabin or the lounge—the guard Captain Rappa had promised—Martha and Claudia were largely alone. There was no Mr. Bindar; there were no veiled women. The captain and the first mate were formally cordial but quick to avoid socialization or further confrontation.

On the second morning, when Nikkos brought them coffee, Martha could see through the open door of the lounge into dazzling sunlight. The Swan II was passing the Rock of Gibraltar. Martha thought of the baboons that lived on its cliffs and felt sure they were far more civilized than most of her shipmates.

Since the captain's visit to their suite two days before, Martha had not slept well or much at all. She was kept awake by the feeling that there was a solution to their dilemma just out of reach. A solution that tantalized her, that beckoned with a promised of security.

But no such solution actually presented itself. And when Martha opened the door for Nikkos that particular morning and saw Gibraltar, it seemed to her a mirage, a huge, granite, unreachable sanctuary.

Nikkos refused to talk, wouldn't even look up from the tray. When Martha told him to put it on the table, he walked like a blind man, finding his way across the lounge without seeing a thing. Claudia was on the couch in front of him, her legs curled up under her white cotton nightdress. When Nikkos put the tray down, Claudia thanked him, and the softness of her voice seemed to be more than Nikkos could bear.

"I get off with you in Turkey," he said. "I never leave again. You stay inside until then. I guard you."

Nikkos held both hands before him, gesturing like a timid faith healer. He looked miserable, his pallid face contorted by emotion, but to Martha he was just another person who needed help, another lost soul on this ship, in short, another problem. And she wasn't in the mood for this addition to her burden. Nor could she shake the unpleasant sensation that the steward wasn't as pathetic as he seemed. She told Nikkos that all would be fine and that he could leave, but Nikkos ranted on.

"That poor woman, that poor woman. Why they do that to her? Why she all tied up like that sometimes? Why those women so mean to her? Sometimes they make her crawl around. One woman very mean. They all animals. They take her to Algeria. What for like that? Horrible and horrible."

Martha was exhausted by intrigue. She had as many answers as she needed and more information than she could do anything with. But the implication of Nikkos' hysterical ranting was another sudden thud in her ribs.

Like the captain and no doubt Mr. Bindar, Nikkos, the obsequious steward and fellow uninformed victim, was a liar. That he knew enough about the captive woman to be so specifically histrionic betrayed his innocence. What part he played in this shipboard plague she didn't know, but he seemed to be as infected by dissembling as the rest. Martha had no use for his particular brand of sneakiness.

Nikkos looked like he was about to sit down, to join them in suffering. "Nikkos," Martha said curtly, "I want you to leave now. We want to be alone, so please go."

Martha stood, took Nikkos' arm, and lead him to the door. When she opened it, she saw that Gibraltar had slid a bit further back along the rail, even further out of reach.

"We don't mean to be rude," Claudia called out, "but we're just so tired of the whole horrible situation. Do you understand?"

Martha saw the dark, mean look flash into Nikkos' eyes and then it was gone. He bowed, and hurried off.

Claudia uncurled herself from the couch and leaned forward to pour herself some coffee. "We have one friend on this ship," she said petulantly, "and you don't have to be rude to him."

Martha walked over to her companion and asked for her hand. Claudia gave it. Martha took it in both of hers, kissed it, then held it against her cheek. "We have no friends on this ship," she said solemnly, "except each other. And we'll take care of each other, won't we?"

Claudia's eyes softened with love and with trust. "I'm sorry, darling," she whispered. "I'm just so scared and I don't want to be." And then she started to cry.

By late morning it was warm enough to sit on lounge chairs on deck. Claudia was exhausted and tense; she did nothing more strenuous than look at the shipping traffic, which had dramatically increased since the Swan II had entered the Mediterranean. At noon she asked for a Bloody Mary and after a second, began to feel relaxed. She noted that the air was different here, drier, more like licorice than salt. She watched sea birds soar and dive, and flying fish leap and dart. She spotted a cruise ship far off the port side and for crazy moment considered jumping up and down at the rail to get its attention, considered shouting "Get us off of this horrible ship!"

But she didn't jump and cry for rescue. Claudia believed that the Swan II was moving closer to civilization. Claudia believed that she and Martha were moving inexorably closer to land and to safety.

Finally, Claudia moved her lounge chair up against Martha's, rolled onto her side, and sank into a sound sleep.

Both women had double Scotches at cocktail hour, enjoyed a game of Scrabble, and shared the relief of having gotten through a day without incident.

"Maybe we can't save that poor young woman," Martha told Claudia as they prepared for dinner. "But surely we can save ourselves."

They ate alone in the lounge, and when Nikkos served them, he made eye contact with neither. But he did have a small envelope and when Martha reached to retrieve a napkin that had fallen to the floor, he palmed it into Claudia's hand. She looked up at him inquisitively; Nikkos put his finger to his lips, letting her know that whatever was in the envelope was their secret. Claudia nodded and slipped it under the napkin on her lap.

After dinner, while Martha excused herself to visit the ladies' room, Claudia read the note.

If you want return present, meet me in the kitchen at 2:00 in the tomorrow afternoon. It will be safe. Only you come, please. Nikkos

The anklet, or rather, the fetter. It was unfinished business. Its meaning was so distasteful that Martha and Claudia had put it away with no further discussion except that once they reached Turkey it would be given over to the captain with the request that he return it to the prince's family. That Nikkos had perhaps arranged a more direct way of returning it was perfect. Now there was even the possibility of learning whom, exactly, among the prince's party, had given it.

Not for one second did Claudia stop to wonder how Nikkos knew about the fetter. She trusted him. By the time Martha returned to the lounge, Claudia was already figuring out how to get away at two o'clock, "tomorrow in the afternoon."

CHAPTER 16

Long before they could see port, Martha and Claudia could smell it: petroleum, fetid garbage, human waste. The stench was in the air when they woke up, and when land began to appear ahead, a leprous sore on the horizon, it suggested no promise of relief. Instead it offered yet another, albeit terrestrial, version of purgatory.

As the Swan II drew closer to shore, three knots per hour across the River Styx, Ghazaouet's grimness grew into sharper focus, floating out to greet them in greasy slicks of curious debris, bobbing chemical drums, blue-green-yellow suds, a bloated goat carcass, plastic and wood and Styrofoam long peeled away from recognizable use.

The Slave Coast.

Martha knew about Algeria, about the hundreds of thousands of slaves who passed through ports along this coast, lost to home and family forever. Now the horror of historical association was converted to physical revulsion.

By eleven o'clock the morning air was already suffocating. *We're being drawn into a Dali painting*, Martha thought as she watched the boil of land infect and swell as they got closer. Off the starboard side a tire floated by and attached to it, by a wire around its neck, was a human corpse.

Claudia stood by Martha on the bow and watched the shore with dreadful fascination.

The three docks were largely deserted, bomb craters interrupting two of them from connecting land to sea. The third had collapsed short of the water by about thirty yards. Barges had been tied end to end so that at least one dock was serviceable. Two marine derricks squatted on this third dock, collapsed and crumpled like huge melted prostheses. Off the starboard side a freighter was hopelessly aground on a breakwater, its exposed hull rusted and pitted like the surface of Mars. A listing dhow was tied to it; someone on board, dark and naked, was trying to remove rivets from the freighter's skeleton rudder. On the shore a single warehouse remained. It had been reduced to two walls of re-bar and concrete, and inside a fire smoldered, smoke rising into even fouler air. Everywhere gulls and vultures circled overhead, wafting on the stink of carrion treasures.

At two o'clock, just as a pilot boat from somewhere was motoring out to them across the foul water, Claudia excused herself, promising Martha that she would be right back. She hurried along the portside deck to their cabin and went in to get the anklet. She opened Martha's dresser drawer and lifted up the box, surprised again by how heavy it was. She didn't open it one last time. She never, ever, wanted to see it again.

Claudia left the cabin, noting with a tiny part of her consciousness that their guard was not on duty, and walked back towards the stern to the kitchen.

The Filipino kitchen staff was gone. A huge pot of chicken soup was simmering on the range and cantaloupes had been split and left on the chopping block in the middle of the room. Nikkos was sitting on a stool, next to a mixer that was almost as tall as he was.

He looked as scared as he always did, but Claudia noticed that the wide, child-like desire to please was gone from his eyes, replaced, she thought, by something rat-like. She began to feel that being there alone with him was a mistake.

"Nikkos," she said, holding out the box, "just return this for me, please. I need to get back to Ms. Bekele."

Claudia took a step closer to Nikkos, but instead of reaching for the box he slid off the stool, turned, and opened the door that led to the deck above.

"No," he said, "you come give it to them yourself. I promise you would. The women, they want to see you before they leave. They like you. Mr. Bindar and captain left on small boat, gone for a while. No worry. Come."

There was a whining surliness in the man's voice that Claudia almost found amusing; it was almost like a child's plaintive whine, she thought. But as she drew closer, she smelled the body odor of someone deeply agitated. Suddenly, his eyes were absolutely hateful.

Claudia put the box down next to a deep aluminum sink. "Nikkos," she said, aware of the tremor in her voice, "I will have nothing more to do with this. This matter is over and you are not to mention it again. Goodbye."

She turned and started for the door to the deck when she heard Nikkos call to someone, not in Greek, she realized, but in the sputtering consonants of Arabic. And then he was in front of her, blocking the door to the deck.

Claudia was a foot taller than Nikkos and probably stronger, and for a moment she found his refusing to let her pass absurd. Until she saw the knife in his hand. She whirled around towards the thundering of footsteps behind her and saw three women in western dress. Before she could react, they were on her. Two pulled her arms painfully up behind her back and the third, holding a long silk wrap, grabbed her by the hair and with the other hand forced a large knot in the middle of the scarf into her mouth. Claudia twisted desperately but soon she was gagged, the scarf tied so tightly around her head that she thought her mouth would split open.

The women forced her up the narrow stairway to the deck above. She tried to fight, to twist herself away from her captors, but arched backwards by the wrenching pressure on her arms and with the ends of the scarf being used like reins, her attempts to break free were futile and excruciating.

When they got to the deck above, the women hustled Claudia into the cabin where everything looked all too familiar: the Persian rug, the giant pillows around its perimeter. The young, bound woman Claudia had found there was nowhere to be seen, but Claudia's terror was amplified by the awful memory of the woman's pleading eyes.

One of the women tripped her and Claudia would have fallen on her face except for the woman behind holding her back by the ends of the gag. Still, she was on the floor, face down, and felt her wrists and elbows being bound by one of the women while another kneeled on the small of her back. Finally, they rolled her onto her back and Claudia kicked out until the women caught her legs and held them straight out, pinned to the floor.

And then Claudia watched in horror as one woman took the anklet from Nikkos. Making sure that all the precious stones were facing out, the woman carefully locked the bejeweled fetter into place with a click, then tugged it hard to make sure it was secure. She then fastened another plain anklet around Claudia's other ankle and joined them together by a short chain.

Claudia was exhausted, the fight burned out of her. And in that lull when struggle becomes resignation, she looked up at her four kidnappers with wide, terrified eyes and in the only way she could, asked why.

The only answer was the clucking of a mysterious language as they stood staring down at her.

The large powerful woman seemed also the oldest. Claudia had seen the dark hair that at this woman's wrists when she was struggling against being gagged, and now that she could see her face, noticed its crude, over-sized features and the fine, black hair that was making incursions into it, too, bridging eyebrows, sketching in a mustache, forming little quills on her chin. Claudia looked down from the ugly face to the woman's oversized sweatshirt. In bold letters the sweatshirt announced "Disneyworld". Claudia looked back up, right into the woman's eyes, hoping that this small piece of shared information would somehow make things better between she and her captor. Claudia looked down again at the logo, then back to the woman. She nodded, even though the gag pulled at the corners of her already sore mouth.

The coarse featured woman smiled and nodded back. For a split second Claudia allowed herself to feel hope—until the woman suddenly bent over, ripped open Claudia's blouse, forced her hands up underneath Claudia's bra, and squeezed her nipples. Claudia arched in pain; she heard herself make an unrecognizable sound past the silk gag, a deep sound that filled the room with agony and humiliation. Before the woman stood up, she patted Claudia on the cheek with mock affection, and stroked the gag with false tenderness.

Claudia rolled off her hands onto her side. She shut her eyes in a vain attempt to make her captors go away, if only for a moment. But then she heard the sound of scissors slicing in the air and her eyes flew open. She watched as the youngest woman, barely twenty, Claudia thought, unfolded a large silken bundle. Nothing that had happened thus far terrified her as much as what was about to happen. Up until that moment Claudia had convinced herself her capture was ultimately a game, a prank, albeit a brutal one, staged by strange, spoiled girls at ugly play. Claudia's spirit had survived by believing that her misery would soon come to an end.

But now, the truth was clear. These women were going to cut off her own clothes and hide her under an impenetrable veil and yards of formless fabric like those worn by the woman they had forced on board in Boston.

These women were going to take her off the ship.

Claudia strained against her bonds but was bound too tightly and thoroughly to achieve even the slightest bit of freedom. Resigned, she began to cry.

CHAPTER 17

An ancient tug, spewing black clouds of diesel smoke, moved to the starboard side and pushed the Swan II through the oil-slick water towards the barges that served as the water-end of the dock. Pods of dead fish floated past in macabre synchronization and on the shore Martha could see barefooted children fighting for treasures in the rubble. The vultures were lined up on the girders of the twisted cranes, waiting for whatever offal the arrival of the Swan II might offer. There were no other boats, nothing else even moving except for puffs of dust and smoke curling from garbage mounds and pox craters.

Behind the collapsed dock the land rose into rolling hills that were scorched into charcoal ridges, the trees like cigarette butts in a giant landscape ashtray.

Martha had been standing alone on the bow for forty minutes, watching this grimness draw near. She hadn't blamed Claudia for retreating from it and wondered why she herself persisted the morbid staring. She tried to imagine what circumstances in the infinite versions of political horror could have created this place, and she shuddered at what must be waiting here for the young woman Claudia had seen tied in the cabin. As she stared ashore, any lingering disbelief in the darkness of the world abated.

She turned from the rail to go to Claudia, whom she assumed was waiting in their cabin. She wanted to wrap her arms around Claudia and protect her from these kinds of places. But just then something on shore caught her attention. On the road that began as a thread running down from the blackened hills and towards the docks in discontinuous slabs of Macadam, three vehicles approached, giant insects across the wasteland: an old Peugeot, a huge black Mercedes, and last, incredibly keeping up with the other two, a tank. An incongruous procession anywhere else but Algeria, Martha thought, as they pulled up as close to the dock as the road allowed and stopped. A hatch in the tank turret clanked open and a head popped out, its face hidden by helmet and goggles. Martha thought it looked like a praying mantis. The creature crawled up and sat on the rim of the turret, did something with the machine gun that was mounted there, and then lifted his goggles and lit a cigarette.

This was the receiving end of what had begun with Mr. Bindar and company in Boston. Martha nearly laughed as she thought of what her advertising firm would have to do to sell this trip: "Exotic ports of call will feature a forbidden dock in Algeria where passengers can thrill to the dramatic clash of diverse religions, tribes, even nations. If we're lucky, we'll actually see history being made."

Martha turned away from this bizarre scene to find Nikkos just behind her, out of breath and more agitated than she had ever seen him.

"Miss Bekele, something happen to cello. This is very bad. Please come. I don't know what to do."

"Let's go, Nikkos," Martha said. As she followed the little man she thought about Claudia's cello. Claudia had bought it by bid from a dealer in Munich almost three years earlier. The cello was an Amati and had cost a quarter of a million dollars. Although she had neglected to play it regularly, not because of a lack of interest but rather because of a too busy schedule, Claudia loved the instrument dearly. It had become her cumbersome, fragile companion. That she had brought the cello on this trip at all seemed to Martha another instance of the very kind of irresponsibility that, ironically, made Claudia so dear. Claudia had insisted that being able to spend four uninterrupted weeks of playing for Martha was the best use she could ever imagine for it.

"I want you to hold its sound," Claudia had said, "the way I do. Intimately." And so transporting the priceless cello had meant abandoning it for hours at a time, trusting bellhops and cab drivers and longshoreman and Swan II crewmen in greasy blue coveralls with its care. Claudia's cello was nothing less than a miracle of fragile durability, a centuries-old gift to the human spirit.

Nikkos led Martha back towards the stern. They reached a door marked "Maintenance" above the international no-smoking symbol. It was a watertight door, one of hundreds on the ship. What Claudia's cello was doing in a maintenance room increased Martha's feelings of anxiety. As soon as Nikkos had opened the heavy door, Martha stooped through and was in.

The space was dim. The only light came through the doorway behind them, but Martha could see there was nothing in the room except cans and drums of solvent and paint. Martha looked at Nikkos, puzzled, but Nikkos moved ahead to another watertight door and turned the wheel latch to open it. This room was even darker and entering it, Martha could tell it wasn't much bigger than a closet—and that the cello was not in here, either. Exasperated, she turned to question Nikkos just as the door clamped shut behind her with a heavy clang. And then she could hear the first door through which they had come clang close, too.

For a moment Martha was too shocked to move, her eyes frozen on the steel door in front of her. But when her dumbfounded paralysis had lifted, she leapt for the door, pulled at it, and screamed for Nikkos.

But she knew that nobody could hear her.

CHAPTER 18

The women stood Claudia on her feet where she balanced precariously, ankles chained closely together. Naked except for bra and panties, she shrank as the women touched her skin, felt the satin of her bra, fussed admiringly with her hair. While the youngest woman smoothed out the burqua and carefully gathered it up into folds, the other woman, maybe Claudia's age, pulled the lace elastic band of Claudia's silk panties away from her stomach and looked down into her crotch. Then she laughed and let the elastic snap back. Claudia shook her head and tried to protest but the muffled whimper made her feel even more humiliated.

The youngest woman approached her and fitting the hood end of the burqua over her head so the little cage of fine mesh was in front of her face, dropped the garment down and smoothed it in place. It hung to the ground like a voluminous silken sack. Claudia could feel its soft weight pull at her head as it fell, and she tried again in spite of the gag to say "no," and "please." This time she got a response. While the woman was making the garment fit, squaring the shoulders, pulling at the hem, adjusting the fitted hood just so, Claudia heard her whisper in fractured French.

"I am so sorry I have to do this to you."

Through the little cage of her veil, Claudia tried to see what she was becoming, but her head turned against the weight of the material, away from the mesh opening. By the time she had learned to shift her head so that it moved with its covering, the women had finished their task. What Claudia could finally see was the three women staring at her, transfixed by the utter, transformed helplessness of their captive.

CHAPTER 19

Martha was no longer scared. She knew that eventually someone would find her, but she had to do something with her anger and frustration. She grabbed a paintbrush and banged its wooden handle against the door, the walls, and by standing on a large drum, the ceiling.

She believed she knew perfectly what was happening, that she and Claudia, prisoner somewhere else on the ship, were being locked away until that poor girl had been taken off by Mr. Bindar and his shrouded hags. Nikkos would come back for her when it was all over, and Martha looked forward to slapping his servile face.

Martha stopped banging and sat down on a coil of thick electrical hoses connected to something that looked like a jackhammer. She had spent enough time in her life waiting, albeit usually in VIP lounges of airports, that in some respects this was just another inconvenience. Dealing with the captain and the rest of the circumstances of the voyage from hell would have to wait until they got to the embassy in Turkey, but she was pretty sure that in all of this there could be a Pulitzer Prize for Claudia: "American Conspiracy in International Kidnapping." And the lawsuit against the steamship company would be magnificent. In fact, a year from now, Martha mused, the Swan II could be renamed, "Martha's Claudia."

Then it would be a happy ship.

CHAPTER 20

Claudia sat on the edge of the bed, her posture rigid because of the way she was bound underneath the maroon burqua that covered her from head to toe. She noticed that it was perfumed, Chanel #5 she thought, and the pleasant familiarity of the cool scent that covered her face and engulfed her body tantalized her with recollections of normalcy. Inexplicably, she remembered the gray taffeta gown she had worn twenty years before to the Gothems at the Waldorf Astoria. She was still in college, young and looking forward to the rest of her life. She remembered the hansom cab ride through Central Park after the event, warm in the depths of her mother's fur coat. She remembered how vividly the snowflakes were defined as they fell on the tartan lap robe the driver had insisted that she wear. She remembered, too, her date, a cadet from West Point, talking about the Crimean War, and how bored she was with him and how in love she was with the elegant black girl in her class who wore the Radcliff uniform of a pleated skirt and sweater and pearls but whose hair was cut so short she looked like a late dynasty Egyptian goddess.

Claudia's reverie was shattered when two men came into the cabin with hand trucks. They were bare footed, had unevenly shaved heads, and wore dirty robes. They loaded the hand trucks with trunks and boxes, passing back and forth across the room directly in front of Claudia several times. Claudia tried to get their attention by twisting and making pleading, nasal noises past the gag. They didn't even glance at her, probably, she knew, from years of conditioning forbidding them to recognize the presence of women.

The men had been gone about five minutes when Nikkos came into the room pushing an old, wicker wheel chair with a high back and over-sized wooden wheels. It reminded Claudia of something out of a grim, Victorian-era sanitarium. Everything about the chair was dreadful. Claudia again tried to squirm free but succeeded only in amusing Nikkos.

"No want to go for ride, beautiful Miss Claudia?" Nikkos wheeled the chair right in front of her and patted the seat. "For beautiful Miss Claudia, very special." He walked around and groped for where he thought Claudia's crotch might be underneath the burqua's folds and pleats. "I fuck you later," he whispered.

Claudia could smell him, see his ferret eyes; she hoped he saw her own eyes through the mesh, hoped he could saw the loathing and disgust she had for him. "God, at least give me that," she thought.

Suddenly, Nikkos left and she was by herself again, unable to move, alone in her personal tent that muffled sound and sight and, because it was perfumed, even her sense of smell. She wondered where Martha was right then, if she was looking for her, if she was all right. She wondered why she hadn't seen the other young woman whom she had found captive days ago. And she wondered where Mr. Bindar was, the monster who should have scared her enough to stay away from these brutal people.

The three women returned. The one with the DisneyWorld sweatshirt and the other, not the young one who had whispered to Claudia in French, grabbed Claudia, lifted her into the wheel chair, and held her there against the wicker.

Claudia refused to struggle any longer. She knew it was both futile and humiliating. When the French- speaking woman took leather straps and secured her ankles and neck to the back of the wheel chair, Claudia thought it was almost gentle.

CHAPTER 21

Martha estimated that she had been locked in the little maintenance room for about three hours. It was hot and the smell of paint and solvents was making her sick, eroding her resolve to stay calm. She had found an overhead light, and even though it was just a single, low-wattage bare bulb, it allowed her to look around for something that would make more noise than a wooden paintbrush handle, maybe an iron bar or a hammer. But there was nothing except the jackhammer connected in some way to the hoses she had been nesting on and another strange looking device, like an oversized lawn mower. Its casing declared it an Arnessen Deck Scaler.

Martha couldn't budge the deck scaler, but she could lift a smaller version of the jackhammer she found next to it. By resting the smaller machine on a cardboard box, Martha could place its thin, sharp head perpendicularly against the door, as if she were preparing to drill through. Martha followed the machine's hoses to an air compressor and sought its power source. She remembered the other name for jackhammer, "pneumatic drill," and understood the relationship between the drill and the compressor. After fifteen minutes of trial and error, the compressor was going, filling the room with suffocating diesel fumes.

Martha walked back to the jackhammer, found a little trigger by the handles, and, bracing herself, started it up. The machine jumped out of her hands. She lifted it back onto the cardboard box and leaning against it, her feet braced, pulled the trigger.

The jackhammer was deafening by itself, but when she engaged it against the door, the room exploded into demented metallic pounding. It was excruciating and Martha stopped immediately to look for pieces of material she could make into ear plugs. She found nothing. Finally, she reached behind her neck, tore out the labels of her dress, and rolled them into little cones. The she tamped them as deeply into her ears as she could: "100% Pure Cashmere," in one; "Paul of San Francisco," in the other.

She started the jackhammer again. The din was still agonizing and it shook her violently; Martha felt as if her teeth, arms, all her organs were being shaken loose from her body. She felt suffocated by the paint fumes and diesel exhaust and fought to remain conscious. She was determined to remain on her feet as long as she could and keep the jackhammer pounding the door, turning the tiny room into a metal, cacophonous amplifier.

Just when she could stand neither the sound nor the smell any longer, she saw the wheel on the door move. The jackhammer dropped to the floor and a mate stood in the doorway, dressed formally in a Swan II blue uniform.

CHAPTER 22

Had the captain or the first mate or Martha been on deck hours earlier, they would have seen a strange procession moving down the gangplank, three women in burqua gliding like wraiths, each step identified by a puff of the material which hung in volumes around their ankles, followed by three barefooted men, two with laden hand trucks and the third carrying an awkward case which looked big enough to hold a cello.

Behind this procession came another woman, also completely swathed in yards of maroon material, sitting in an old wheel chair. Once, she arched her body forward, but her head and feet seemed attached somehow to the chair and after her mid-section had bowed forward, she didn't move again. Guiding the wheel chair and struggling with its weight down the incline was a little man who even from the distance of the deck sixty feet above would have looked nervous and servile and thoroughly evil.

CHAPTER 23

As soon as she was on deck, Martha was sick. Her head pounded so violently she couldn't hear what the mate was saying, nor she could she hear herself ask again and again for Claudia.

The mate gently took her to her suite and waited outside the bathroom door while she cleaned up. When she came out, the ringing in her ears had abated enough so that she could hear herself speak though her voice, for the first time she could remember, was edged with panic.

"Get Claudia," she said. "I want Claudia. Please. She's somewhere on this ship, maybe locked away, too. Get her. Please. Now."

"The captain has just returned on board," the mate told her, clearly frightened by her urgency. "I'll get him straight away. Don't worry."

When he had gone, Martha sat on the bed, engulfed by an emotion she barely even understood: hopelessness.

Minutes later someone knocked at the door, startling her. She leapt up, crossed the little suite, and tore open the door. There, filling the bulkhead door frame, was Mr. Bindar.

It was five steps back to the little bedside table. Five steps and Martha held the silver .380 automatic cocked and, using two hands as she had been trained to do, aimed right at Mr. Bindar's chest.

The gun seemed to have no impact on Mr. Bindar. He looked at her almost kindly, and said, "I don't mean to frighten you, although I know a face like mine frightens."

Martha held the gun steady. "Where is Claudia?" she demanded. "Let her out right now." Martha hoped it would be this simple, that minutes from now she and Claudia would be together, safe, and soon, sailing away from this horrible place.

With a surprising gentleness in his voice that Martha found disconcerting, Mr. Bindar continued. "Miss Bekele, I am Mr. Abbas

Bindar, a policeman with the DGSN, the Algerian government. Miss Simmerhorn is not on this ship. I have been looking, too, but it seems she was taken off when the others left. And now there is trouble."

Martha was wracked by a wave of nausea and by the vertigo of complete disbelief. She felt as if she were watching this scene in the movie of her life from the balcony of a spinning theater. The little gun in her hand was a silly movie prop. She felt the room twirl and knew if she didn't sit down she would be sprawled on the floor, retching again.

She backed up towards the bed, her hands shaking but the gun still aimed at Mr. Bindar. Suddenly, the door framed a second person, someone dressed like the captain of a ship. Martha sat on the edge of the bed and pointed the gun at the floor. And then she was sobbing.

"Give me Claudia" she cried, "please give me my Claudia."

The captain awkwardly put out his hand out as if offering to hold hers.

"Ms. Bekele," he said softly, "Mr. Bindar and I have been trying to protect you and Ms. Simmerhorn. We…"

Martha's despair erupted into rage. "Mr. Bindar assaulted Claudia, kept a young woman bound in her room, and you, Captain Rappa, have protected him, not me or my companion. You are accomplices, not in any way allies of mine. And don't think I am stupid, and don't think I am without resources. You may be in charge of a ship but you will find it very hard to sail through the trouble I intend to cause unless Claudia is back with me immediately. Take this very seriously, Captain. And don't try to tell me Mr. Bindar is my friend."

Martha's anger was momentarily exhausted and when she asked again, "Where is Claudia?" there was desperation in her voice.

As if recognizing that the fight was out of Martha, the captain asked gently, "Ms. Bekele, please, may I speak for a moment?"

Martha put the gun on the floor and her elbows on her knees, then, cradled her head in her hands. She nodded for Captain Rappa to continue.

"You and Ms. Simmerhorn should never have been allowed on this ship. Had I known all the circumstances of this passage, I would have put you off immediately. Mr. Bindar, to his credit, was the only person who told me the truth about Prince Jed al Hann, whose family we regretfully have had on board, and that was only when we were far out to sea."

Martha continued to stare at the floor. "Maybe," she said acridly, "Mr. Bindar was the one who should have been taken off the ship. Ever thought of that, captain? Or were his cigars too good."

"Mr. Bindar," Capatain Rappa went on calmly, "tried to frighten you and Ms. Simmerhorn away from those people. That's why he left the room where the young woman was being kept unlocked. He knew that Ms. Simmerhorn was curious and hoped that if she came upon the unfortunate woman she would realizes that the business on A deck was nasty. That is also why he was a bit rough with her. To scare her."

Martha was disgusted by this defense. She looked up at the captain. "Beating people scares them, all right," she said. "What he did to Claudia bloody scared her. What he did to Nikkos scared her, too. Was Mr. Bindar just practicing on him when he blackened both his eyes?"

Mr. Bindar, who had remained standing by the door, now stepped fully into the room. His voice was cold.

"Nikkos Lindos is from Carpathos," he said. "I will tell you about him."

Martha didn't want to hear anything more from Mr. Bindar, but a look from Captain Rappa stopped her protest.

"He calls himself The Mahdi, after an Islamic hero of the Sudan years ago. Miss Bekele, Nikkos is a terrorist. I couldn't believe he was on this ship, part of this sick transaction between your government and mine."

Martha exploded with indignation. "Don't you dare blame this mess on my government!" she cried.

Mr. Bindar ignored her and went on. "Nikkos Lindos. No father, a brother who was a priest, a sister who was killed in a fire when she was twelve. She was changing the water in vases of flowers on a sunny Friday morning in the village church when it exploded into flames. Nikkos' first successful fire, he likes to brag. He was fourteen. He is sick, hates all things but feels more dignified to have a cause so he first chooses to hate Greek Orthodoxy. Two old priests die, his mother's ribs kicked in for praying, another church burned, others ransacked. He runs out of weak targets and leaves his town. After he kills his brother with a knife."

Martha stared at Mr. Bindar in disbelief. She and her beloved Claudia had spoken with, even felt sorry for this exemplar of evil.

"He needs more things to hate," Mr. Bindar went on, "and finds a fundamentalist Islamic sect, perfect because it hates everything. Now he feels dignified because this Islamic group gives him small projects but he feels his cause is big and he is big hero. He blows up a store in Lebanon, throws firebomb into bus in Damascus, was leading the mob who stoned a girl to death in Tamanrasset, in my country, for not observing Hijab, the code that requires Muslim women to cover themselves. She was fifteen-years old. He later went to the girl's home and raped her sister. With a stick. Then he gets a job as guard on this boat for Prince's family, and part of the filthy business is that he is to be employed as steward so he can spy on other passengers. Your country arranged that quite nicely."

Again there was the insinuation that her country might have some complicity in what had happened on board, but this time Martha didn't have the impulse to protest.

"I don't apologize for hitting him," Mr. Bindar said. "I apologize for not killing him. When I find out my country is using him for this, when I see him on this ship, when I realize, I try to keep you away from him, try to scare you and Miss Simmerhorn away without giving up my country's and your country's bad secret. Now, I have failed at everything."

There was genuine sorrow in the big man's eyes and Martha, looking intently at him now, was struck by this.

"What bad secret?" she asked, hearing a softness in her voice. Martha had the absurd thought that she was in a room full of victims, experiencing group therapy for the emotionally shanghaied.

"Algeria has no history of peace," Mr. Bindar told her then. "It has been at war with others and itself throughout most of the century. As a consequence it is a dangerous, violent country but because of its geographic position on the Mediterranean, it is a country that, while hard to like, is even harder to leave alone. Russia can't, France can't, Libya can't and, why we are in this mess now, your country can't."

As Mr. Bindar's discourse veered into a lesson on international relations, Martha's feelings of helplessness grew. Claudia seemed to become smaller, a threadbare figure in the corner of a contemporary tapestry depicting Armageddon.

"The Algerian government is trying for internal peace," Mr. Bindar went on. "One group that has caused continual and barbaric unrest is the Groupe Islamic Armee, the GIA. It wants Algeria to be fundamentalist Islamic State, no constitution, just the Koran. The Algerian government tries to placate them, tries to negotiate, but they bomb and kill and refuse chances for peace.

"Then Algerian government tries so hard, so often, the GIA sees chance for outrageous, sometimes bizarre concessions. A gold roof for a minaret in El Golea, open doors for all the prisons, an invasion of Tunisia, a national tribunal for crimes against Islam, holy palaces built into the side of the Hoggar Mountains, a new car, two new cars—a black one and a white one. The list is long.

"Some concessions they get. Like this one." Here Mr. Bindar produced from an inside pocket of his jacket a parchment document. "Do you read French, Miss Bekele?" Mr. Bindar asked as he handed it to her.

Martha nodded but felt too desperate to concentrate on the document, other than to note that it was of a legal nature and notarized by both embossed and wax seals. "Can't you just tell me about it?" she pleaded, her eyes brimming with tears. "I want Claudia. That's all. After that, the lesson on world politics will be fine." She looked at the captain. "Radio for help," she begged. "Do something. For the first time, do something to really help, can't you, please?"

"Ms. Bekele," the captain replied gently, "please, let Mr. Bindar continue. What he has to say will affect what we do next."

Martha nodded and Mr. Bindar, after taking back the document, pressed on. "This document is a request by my government that your government assist us in locating and returning the daughter of Prince Jed al Hann to Algeria where she is wanted for treason and 'heinous high crimes against the Democratic and Popular Republic of Algeria.'"

"The young woman Claudia found tied in the cabin," Martha said quickly.

Mr. Bindar nodded. "Do you want to know what her high, heinous crimes were? Adultery. She had an affair and ran away, to safety, to the United States."

"Oh," Martha said.

"For some Muslims," Mr. Bindar explained, "the adultery of a daughter is the worst kind of dishonor. It shames the family forever unless the daughter is punished. Severely. Sometimes by banishment, sometimes by amputation or disfigurement, most often by death. Only then can the family's honor be restored and can they entertain friends or raise their heads in pride at the souks.

"Prince Jed al Hann," Mr. Bindar explained, "lives far inside my country, away from the coast and anything European. He is very wealthy and is a fundamentalist. He gives millions of francs to the GIA, arming terrorist and, we think, coordinating their activities. He also has alliances with Libya, another of our enemies. He is very powerful and very bad for Algeria."

Martha nodded, though the details of Mr. Bindar's story were barely registering in her tired brain.

"The prince has three daughters," Mr. Bindar went on. "Nura, the middle daughter, betrayed him. She was a princess, of course a Muslim, and had been married for three years, since she was seventeen. She was on holiday in Tunisia, out of the oda for the first time in months, and met a young American man who was teaching some farmers in a village below the palace of her hosts how to work a tractor.

"She had watched him from her window for days and one evening, just before dusk—the time when he usually stopped, the time when he could be counted on to come out of the rust fields of milo on his green tractor—she left the palace, not even caring enough to hide her face behind a veil.

"Nura was refined, spoiled, very pretty, used to getting what she wanted. I guess your compatriot thought she was exotic."

The word "compatriot" again made Martha wonder if she was supposed to feel guilty, as if somehow by also being an American she was complicit in Nura's downfall.

Mr. Bindar continued. "They had sex. She ran away with him, to Oregon. And Prince Jed al Hann lost a daughter and all dignity to the worse kind of infidel, one who was both Christian and American.

"So, the prince says to our president, 'You bring back my daughter from America and the GIA will stop all killing in the Plateau of Chasams.' And our president calls your president and says, 'One of your Peace Corps Workers has run off with a princess and if you can help bring her back we will negotiate a way to control our petroleum refining wastes in the Mediterranean with you.'

"And your president says, 'We will get her back to you but this is our secret.' And so the best way to keep a secret is to kidnap Nura and hide her behind a veil on a small freighter and take her to a port that has been destroyed for years. Except…"

Martha could tell by Mr. Bindar's hesitation that his story was finally coming to a close. As eager as she was to know all there was to know, she dreaded what he was going to say next.

"Except Nura never makes it all the way. She is thrown overboard by Nikkos and the others, drowned, and, now this is what I think happened, the women take Miss Simmerhorn instead. Prince Jed al Hann wants revenge, a beautiful replacement, ideally an American, to regain his honor. That's what I think happened to Miss Simmerhorn."

Somewhere outside in the stink and haze of the evening a tin bell rang dully, the clapper rocked in a current or tide. Water trickled into the sea from the bilge, and, far away, faint, muffled explosions rolled over charred hills. Martha's cries were lost in the smoke-stained air.

CHAPTER 24

Mr. Bindar returned from the radio room with a message from his government promising that it would do everything it could to locate and rescue Miss Simmerhorn. In the meantime, the Swan II was ordered to be out of port and into international waters within five hours.

Captain Rappa brought back from the radio room an assurance that the United States government, through its embassies in Tunisia and Niger, would file an official protest and demand the return of the kidnapped American. Both embassies denied adamantly that the United States had been a party to a clandestine extradition of the princess and lectured the captain about taking tourists to dangerous countries.

To Martha, it was clear that nothing was going to be done, and that all too soon the Swan II would be out to sea, leaving Claudia farther and forever behind.

At eleven o'clock p.m., an Algerian gunboat appeared to make sure the Swan II would soon get underway. At eleven forty-five, the hawsers were hauled aboard and coiled neatly on the deck, a bell signaled "slow astern" in the engine room, and the ancient tug nosed the Swan II away from the makeshift dock. Twenty minutes later there was a single, melancholy blast from the Swan II's horn when, fully under its own steam, it left the ruined port of Ghazaouet behind.

From the shore Martha and Mr. Bindar watched it go, the flood lights on its deck becoming fainter, the Swan II looking like a small city sinking into the sea.

And then they were alone on the Slave Coast.

PART II

LAND

CHAPTER 1

Once they had left the coastal hills and the small, residually European whitewashed towns that were built no farther than the cool refuge of the marine climate, and once they had passed through the wind-swept desolation of the Atlas Mountains, the land sloped down, vegetation became sparse, faded, and finally vanished into rock and dust and heat. And still the land sloped downwards until it leveled into to a bench, below which stretched the unbroken, vast Sahara, unrelieved until it dissolved into solar haze somewhere at the edge of the earth.

On this tableau of nothingness were barely distinguishable smudges of green, brief, short brush strokes, splattered mistakes. Far away one of these would be the Oasis of Djanet, the fortress of Prince Jed al Hann, where, Martha and Mr. Bindar assumed, Claudia was being kept.

They had been traveling for four days. As soon as the ship had left the port at Ghazaouet, Mr. Bindar had commandeered an old Citroen from somewhere among the scattered concrete buildings standing inland a few hundred yards from port. Hours later Martha and Mr. Bindar were in the town of Mohammadia, at the Auberge Soleil, a plaster building whose patches of skeletal chicken wire and bullet holes loosened its hold on colonial French charm.

In Mohammadia, while Martha waited in a bare, pastel-washed room of a small hotel, watching the fan wobble in the high ceiling, Mr. Bindar prepared them for the descent away from the coastal fragments of western civilization, and into the strictures of Islamic fundamentalism and the raw accommodations of untenable country.

Martha noticed that everybody in the town seemed afraid of or impressed by Mr. Bindar. Whether he was negotiating with civilized discourse or belligerent yelling, the response was always deep salaaming and servility.

Martha, too, found herself giving in to Mr. Bindar's orders. He was going to help find Claudia. Clearly, no other person would. She was uncharacteristically dependent now, and she fought her sense of helplessness with the dim hope that it would be worth it. For the moment she was to stay mostly out of sight, for her own safety. She was a tall, svelte black women dressed in Western clothes in a crumbling village where there didn't seem to be any women at all, and the robed men sitting at the rickety wooden tables in the little dining room of their hotel gawked and laughed openly whenever she appeared. Martha felt—and was—pyrotechnically conspicuous.

In two days Mr. Bindar had secured an old four-wheel drive Toyota Land Cruiser with fifty extra gallons of gasoline stored in jerry cans on the roof; food; gallons of water in bright blue jugs; a case of 9mm. ammunition; bedding; and bundles of clothes wrapped in brown paper as if they had just come back from the laundry.

By the third night on land they had left farms and the possibility of irrigation far behind and after hours of driving through a landscape of rocks and gravel, they slept on the floor of a carpenter's shop in suffocating heat and swarms of flies. Mr. Bindar showed Martha how to roll out the mats they had brought and wrap themselves in sheets, like shrouds, against the flies and against the wisps of sand that drifted underneath doors and through myriad seams.

Each day travel became more difficult. The roads turned from asphalt to gravel to dirt to poorly marked traces over which various attempts at primitive but ingenious roadwork had been tried, sometimes with wooden planks, sometimes with stones, sometimes with concrete or brick. Each material had worked for a few meters or even kilometers before each had failed, and the Toyota would again have to fight for traction in the sand.

Their route south was also punctuated by roadblocks that became more fortified each kilometer south. First, young, barefooted men with rifles, then soldiers with rifles, then bunkers with machine guns and surly, belligerent special police and tanks. At each roadblock papers were handed back and froth, sometimes with laughter, sometimes after maniacal yelling and gesturing, and, Mr. Bindar told Martha, often with directions safely through the thousands of land mines that lay ahead.

After two more days of driving farther and farther south, the roadblocks disappeared, as if not even an armed solider dared to go farther. Martha asked why the roads were empty and Mr. Bindar's reply was grim.

"This is where nobody goes," he said. "This is where the worst of the trouble is. Nobody likes it here."

And each day under Mr. Bindar's guidance, they disappeared further into inconspicuousness. First, Martha in the front passenger seat, dressed conservatively in a long-sleeved blouse and long skirt; Mr. Bindar in the driver's seat in an open shirt and a pair of slacks. Then, Martha wearing a chador and Mr. Bindar a fez. Finally, by the fifth day on the road, Martha heavily veiled in white, as a good Muslim should be, sitting passively in the back seat like a bundle, and Mr. Bindar at the wheel in a robe and dishabba.

As they drove, Mr. Bindar talked to Martha about Muslim dress, about how different countries and different sects interpreted "Hijab," the *Koran's instruction* that women be protected and that men be protected from women. Martha listened.

"For some of us Muslims," he explained, "this simply means women dressing in good taste, avoiding bare shoulders, wearing long dresses, long sleeves. Sometimes covering their head in a chador. But in other places the interpretation is more extreme. When those women, the prince's women, got on the boat they were dressed in burqua, the most conservative covering, where nothing shows. This isn't done in Algeria except when people want to use it to hide like the prince's family did. Burqua is only used in some backward places in Afghanistan and Pakistan, although there are fundamentalists who would like to use it everywhere.

"More typical of conservative Muslim peoples," he went on, glancing at Martha in the rearview mirror, "especially affluent ones like the Saudis, is what you are wearing, a shear veil over the face, a head covering long enough to be a shawl, and an abayya which covers the rest of your body. Less immobilizing than burqua and certainly cooler, but as effective in protecting you from leering eyes. Yes? Believe it or not, some women like it. Not my wife though. She refuses."

Mr. Bindar laughed. Martha wanted to ask him about his wife but didn't. Trying to talk through the veil seemed like too much of a very strange effort.

"When we get further in the south," he said, "you must change again. You'll be able to see better. Down there they wear a niqab, a veil from the bridge of the nose that covers the lower half of the face. That with the head covering which comes down over your forehead, almost to your eyebrows, allows just a little slit in between to see out. And then you wear what they call a "haik," which is like a tent that your whole body disappears underneath so you don't have, how do you say?" There was an awkward silence as Mr. Bindar sought the right words. "Curves or shapes anymore.

"We all try to be good Muslims," he went on, his voice suddenly somehow sad. "Some try too hard. I believe it is the same with some Jews and Christians. They try too hard and do sometimes funny, sometimes ugly things. Isn't that right?"

Martha nodded, causing her veil to billow, and thought of the many ugly things that religion makes people do and how pathetic a veil was against the evil of the world. Still, for the moment she was glad for the anonymity the veil provided in spite of the heat. Silently, she watched the jumble of huge rocks and sand and dunes go by. Each bump in the road jarred the fabric draped over her face, shifting it just enough so she had to refocus, find a new, clearer line of sight. At times, blinking and peering through the veil, she felt disoriented, almost as if she were under water. At those times, her little silver .380 automatic was a comforting lump underneath her abayya.

The next morning Mr. Bindar stopped by a well. Low, scrawny brush surrounded it, and several goats fed on desiccated branches. Suddenly, as if from nowhere, three men approached, trotting almost comically towards the car on scrawny donkeys that had all but disappeared under bundles of sticks and huge, over-stuffed sacks. The donkeys were so small that the feet of the men riding almost dragged along the ground. Following the men was a herd of goats, their eyes shining and curious.

When the men drew closer Martha saw that they were darker than the other people she had encountered since arriving in Algeria. Once they had dismounted, Martha noted that all three were dressed identically. Their heads were wrapped in loose white turbans, with one end hanging under the chin. They wore white, long-sleeved robes that hung to their ankles, and over this, a dark cape, fastened at the neck, that came just inches from the ground.

The men exchanged chehades, ritualized tributes, with Mr. Bindar, and then shook hands in the curious way they did in this part of the country, by lightly brushing palms together repeatedly.

Martha watched from the back seat, forgotten. A breeze came through the open windows of the Land Cruiser so she was comfortable in spite of the sheath of cotton in which she was wrapped. But she knew she would never—could never—get used to the total disregard for a woman's presence in this land. It was as if she had lost absolutely all affect, and to be ignored so thoroughly was maddening.

Yes, Martha thought, maddening was the right word, because crazily, her anger at the absurdity of the situation was infected by a child-like need for any kind of acknowledgment. She was a powerful woman who had been rendered powerless. Not only was she invisible to the rest of the world, but her hearing and vision were muffled by the veil and head covering so that even her own sense of being alive, of being sentient, was dulled.

After the rubbing of hands, Martha watched as the men removed prayer rugs from their donkeys and spread them side by side on the dirt. They took off their shoes and knelt facing east, towards Mecca. She was surprised to see Mr. Bindar do the same, producing his small rug from somewhere beside the car like a magician producing a rabbit from a hat. Since they had been traveling together, Martha had not seen him pause long enough to pray, but now she watched as he joined the three dark men in prayer for what seemed like an interminable time.

Finally, the men rose. Martha was relieved that she and Mr. Bindar could be on their way again, that once again she could speak and act as if she were alive.

But it soon became clear that no one was going anywhere for a while. Martha watched the three men roll up the little prayer rugs and refasten them on the donkeys before untying and removing another bundle. Soon they had a small fire going in the dirt and over this they made tea, boiling water in a blackened kettle before transferring it into an elaborate, shiny brass tea maker. After it had steeped, the tea was poured with great ceremony and precision from three feet above into tiny glasses.

Another hour seemed to pass and no one had looked at her, not even Mr. Bindar. The four men continued to sit around what was left of the fire, only occasionally speaking. Finally, one of the three dark men rose and again Martha felt the relief of expected movement and possible company.

Once again, her hopes were dashed. Martha watched in dismay as the man urinated on one of the donkey's legs without the least concern for modesty, and then as he detached a small drum from the animal's back. When he returned to the other men, he sat down and, drumming the instrument with great flourishes of his fingertips, began a falsetto wail that barely and only occasionally had tonality. The wail rose and fell in swallowed gutturals and unearthly yodels, as the man beat the drum faster and faster. The other two men began to shriek in precise counterpoint and soon they were all, including Mr. Bindar, chanting and swaying, offering their own primal baying to a landscape of brush and goats, empty sky, empty space.

To Martha, their song sounded at first like demented raving, but soon its plaintive wildness in this uninhabitable place became the canvas for a trance, the completion of abandon that her seclusion in the back seat of the Toyota had began. Slowly, Martha drifted away from Claudia, from the car, from herself. Slowly, she became selfless, a vessel of pure sensation. She felt her body sway underneath the fabric, felt the fabric brush against her face as she rocked, felt the men's animalistic, sliding howls as if they were coming from her own throat.

A fly buzzed loudly before the mesh of Martha's veil and broke the spell. And suddenly, the calm of the trance was replaced by pure rage. That the men had ignored her for so long, prayed, drunk tea, peed, sang, kept her waiting in the car as if she simply didn't exist was inexcusable. Martha fought to get her hands free from underneath the abayya and fumbled for the car door. Her sight impaired by the veil, she tripped and almost fell to the sand. Martha was sorely tempted to rip off the veil and let the three little men see who she really was but resisted, just barely, for Claudia's sake. She covered the twenty feet to where the men were seated quickly, her long strides assertive and athletic. And then she looked down at them, from one man to the next, and then finally to Mr. Bindar. The sight of his ugly, alarmed face was not enough to stop her.

"Enough!" she shouted in French. "You have kept me waiting long enough. Say goodbye to your little desert friends. They can play in the sand by themselves."

As soon as she closed her mouth, Martha knew she had made a terrible mistake. The drummer leaped to his feet and screamed at her. The other two men broke their stunned, open-mouth silence and began to chatter in what Martha thought was an amused way. All three men looked expectantly at Mr. Bindar, and Martha just knew they were expecting him to beat her.

Slowly, Mr. Bindar looked up at Martha. His eyes were filled with resignation and regret. In a terrifyingly soft voice, he spoke in French. "You have no idea," he said, "what you have just done."

The drummer was now no more than six inches from Martha. With his hands and then his fists he made what Martha knew were obscene gestures; his fingers flicked imaginary filth at her. Martha stood absolutely still. Then the man drew closer, until his enraged eyes were only inches from her veil. Martha smelled his smoky odor and felt sick.

Suddenly, as if seeing something dark and powerful and frightening in Martha's own eyes, the man recoiled. For a dread moment he stared at her, then turned and ran for his donkey, shrieking something to his companions that made them jump to their feet and run to their donkeys, too.

As if caught in a nightmare, Martha watched as Mr. Bindar yanked the Uzi out from underneath his robes and in a continual burst of rapid shots, kill the drummer and then the other two dark men. The donkeys jerked and brayed in reaction to the noise. The third man, clinging to his animal's pack for support, finally lost his hold and slid down into the dirt, pulling sacks of dates and pistachios on top of him.

The ringing of gunshots and the insolent stares of goats and donkeys. Martha wasn't standing in the Algerian desert with three dead men almost at her feet. It was lousy theater, that was all, a very bad production. The little drum, upside down in the dirt, was just a silly prop.

Another bag slid loose from the third man's donkey and plopped down into the sand by his crooked, outstretched arm.

Martha watched as Mr. Bindar knelt over the body of the drummer. He turned it over and then let it fall back, face down into the sand. Then he stood and stared over at the bodies of the other two men before turning around to confront Martha. Again his voice was surprisingly soft but unmistakably full of disgust.

"These were not silly nomads, Miss Bekele. Nobody we will meet down here will be silly or primitive or picturesque or rude or even slightly concerned about your dignity. They were Berbers, probably bandits, but certainly good Muslims and very capable of affecting what happens to us everywhere along this route. News in the desert travels faster than we do. And if you care about finding Miss Simmerhorn you will remember this and forget your dignity for the time being. Understand?"

Martha understood. She understood that she had never understood violence before these last moments and that she would have to discover new dimensions of strength in herself if she ever expected to find

Claudia. She understood but she couldn't find the words to let Mr. Bindar know that she did.

Mr. Bindar removed a Klasnikov from underneath a blanket on the back of one of the donkeys. His back was to Martha, but he could not hide his anger and exasperation.

"I do not like killing people," he said. "And I don't want to be killed. This didn't have to happen. You are very far from home, Miss Bekele. Once these people knew that you were an impostor, any kind of impostor, they would have killed you and me. And Miss Simmerhorn, she would never be seen again. You make choices and that is what you must choose between. Three people dead but not you and me. Next time maybe different. You and me dead, because you don't like us. But sometimes, Miss Bekele, we live like we do because we want to live. We don't change all at once because that makes us mad or crazy. So we hope to change things and we don't let ourselves go crazy because someday we think we can live long enough to see change. And you and your friend don't understand."

Martha listened and experienced another emotion she had never really known: shame.

Mr. Bindar removed two more guns from the other donkeys. He then unfastened their pack frames, and let their loads fall on the ground. Mr. Bindar slapped the donkey's flanks, sending them away from the only brush for miles.

Martha watched as next he dragged the three bodies over to the lip of the well and, straining, lifted each one up and over the side. The bodies made no noise as they fell.

Only then did he look again at Martha, and he no longer seemed like an ugly thug; he just seemed very tired and very wise. "Everything is ruined here," he said. "Everywhere everything is ruined. But still we try."

When Martha got into the back seat of the Toyota, she was fully aware of another, almost impossible dimension of what it would take to be strong: The ability to do absolutely nothing at all.

CHAPTER 2

Claudia had learned very little but the basics about the women who daily bound her and guided her and groomed her. Zora, one of the prince's daughters, the heavy, coarse featured one, was mean. Sameera, another daughter and the youngest of the captors, the one who had apologized to her back on the ship in her fractured Frnech, was gentle, almost fawning. And Tahani, a wife of the prince, was largely indifferent.

Altogether, Claudia thought, they were bored, and each woman's boredom and character were reflected in her treatment of their prisoner.

Tahani was in charge, but how her orders were carried out depended on who had been given the order, what each woman most needed. Zora needed a victim. Sameera needed a pet.

Claudia wasn't at all sure what Tahani wanted from her. Mostly, it seemed she simply did not want to be disturbed. But she was also not very good about hiding her fascination for this beauty, and Claudia often found Tahani staring at her, almost as if she were being studied.

Claudia spent her days with the three women in a huge, columned room, the opulent coldness of the tile and mosaic walls and domed ceiling softened by thick Turkish rugs which covered bolsters, lounging platforms, giant pillows, divans, cushions, and every square inch of floor, sometimes in layers two and three deep. There were tables, some quite low to the floor; on most of them sat brass platters of fruit, baskets of flowers, or little bowls of burning incense which filled the room with the odor of musk and myrrh, roses and oranges.

Outside one of the high, latticed windows which dominated two sides of the room, Claudia could see an aviary and hear each morning the sounds she had leaned from vacationing a long time ago in Kenya:

African Rollers, Bee Eaters, and other bright birds taken from their sub-Saharan homes. And in this way each day began with the homesick cheerfulness of bird song.

In the middle of the room was a fountain, its running water, more than precious rugs or priceless mosaics or endangered tropical birds, the most opulent decoration in the oda of Prince Jed al Hann in the Oasis of Djanet.

A tile wall, three feet high, encircled the fountain's pool, and on the outside of this, decorative metal rings had been firmly set, for no particular purpose that Claudia at first could understand. But now, each morning after she was dressed and her hands bound together in front of her by ribbons, Claudia was taken into this room and, by a long chain running from a soft leather collar around her neck, attached to one of the rings.

Zora bound Claudia's hands with yanks and sharp tugs, sometimes wrenching Claudia off her feet in the process. And when she fell, Zora would pull harder, straight up, until Claudia was on her feet and moving over to the little ring in the fountain again.

When Sameera bound Claudia's hands, she worked gently but firmly, smoothing the satin ribbons as she tied. She never looked directly at Claudia; sometimes she apologized and blushed and whispered how sorry she was to have to bind such a beautiful woman as Claudia. Always she finished by tying a tight double knot and an elaborate, decorative bow. Strangely, Sameera's embarrassment and care made Claudia's humiliation all the worse.

The diamond anklet had been left on, now just ornamental. And Claudia could see no reason for the bound hands, the collar, the chain. There was no place to go. The palace was surrounded by high, whitewashed walls, too high to admit escape. Through the latticed windows and up over the walls Claudia could see the tops of palms, the fronds collapsing under heavy bunches of oranges and dates. Once, she had seen two Ibis flying across an orange sky. That was all she knew about the world outside the palace grounds. On the morning of the last day of her journey to the prince's oda, the women had dressed her as usual but before dropping the burqua over her, Tahani had placed a silken hood over her head. Claudia had spent the last two hundred miles of the journey veiled and blindfolded.

Now, there was no veil. Claudia was dressed as they all were, in loose, sheer abayyas of royal blues or deep reds or whites or blacks. And each day when she was taken into the domed room and attached to the fountain, she waited for something to happen, for someone to tell her why she was there and what they were going to do with her. She waited for the young woman, the other captive she had seen back on the ship, to appear. She waited for something to change. She waited for Mr. Bindar or Nikkos or some other vile connection to what had happened on the Swan II to make sense of where she was now.

Mostly, Claudia waited for Martha to come and take her home. And while she waited she spent the days in monotonous hours of lounging, as her captors did, but without the language that would have afforded her some company.

One morning, while Claudia was sitting on the edge of the fountain, Sameera walked idly over and sat next to her. Since arriving at the oda, Claudia had been hoping for the opportunity to speak with Sameera alone—and not while the young woman was binding her hands. Of the three women Sameera seemed the weakest, the most reluctant to be a jailor.

"Sameera." Claudia spoke softly. She tried to ask the question as if in conspiracy with a friend. "Why are they keeping me here?"

Sameera seemed startled, either by the question or by Claudia's nerve in asking one. "Because of the prince," she said, defiantly. "You are to make up for his shame for the bad one. The one we took back from your county. His daughter, my sister."

Claudia knew immediately whom Sameera meant, but was compelled to ask, "Do you mean that poor girl tied up on the ship?"

Sameera's face darkened into a mean scowl. "She was not a poor girl. She was a slut. She disgraced our father, our prince. Before we get her back here so he can punish her, she fights and our special guard catches her and she gets thrown into the sea. So we bring you, instead. Now the prince has honor back."

Horrified, Claudia fought to keep a new level of desperation out of her voice. "Did that horrible man with the scarred face kill her?" she asked.

Sameera shook her head. "He is our enemy," she said vehemently. "He works for the government. He would not have helped us. He would like to see the prince and all of us dead. No, the Mahdi did. Nikkos. That was his job."

Of course, Claudia thought, sickened. The little coward would enjoy that. But she couldn't allow herself to dwell on what Sameera had just told her. She couldn't panic. If she did she wasn't sure she could ever stop crying, and these women, her captors, would react with disgust, not compassion, and their treatment of her would only worsen.

Claudia had to change the subject that was threatening to alienate the one person who might be useful to her. She had an idea. "Sameera," she said, "would you brush my hair?"

Sameera blushed with pleasure and, after what looked like a curtsey, left to ask permission from the older women.

She returned a moment later with a silver hairbrush. She sat on the floor and nervously pulled at the hem of Claudia's abayya. Her voice was barely audible, and with deep embarrassment, she said, "It is a thrill for me to brush your hair. But Zora says if you try to talk to me, I must gag you. I don't want to do that, please."

Once again Claudia felt paralyzed by the conflicting responses of anger and dread. She simply nodded that she understood. Sameera rose and sat next to Claudia on the fountain wall. Delicately, she lifted the strands of Claudia's hair that were caught underneath the leather collar, moved the chain out of the way, and begin to brush. After days of being tugged and ignored, led and shunned, poked and forgotten, after days of strange confinement, Sameera's attention to her hair—the little jabs of pain at snarls and the full, rhythmic strokes in between—was an ecstasy of attention. Soon Claudia closed her eyes and was some place else, remembering the hundreds of times Martha had done this for her.

ACROSS

Not even the snugness of the ribbons that bound her hands or the heavy smell of incense or the shrill music that went on and on from the other side of the doomed room could break this moment of unexpected peace. Claudia rolled her head with Sameera's strokes, even though the collar rubbed roughly against her skin. She felt her body begin to sway underneath the soft abayya, felt her hardened nipples dip into little pools of the cool fabric.

Claudia remembered how Martha playfully patted her seat with the brush whenever she wanted to brush Claudia's hair. She allowed herself the luxurious certainty of knowing that Martha would again, someday, hold her, that all would be right, and she drifted even further into pure sensation.

At some point in this trance Claudia opened her eyes and saw Tahani sitting across the room on a low divan, staring at her in utter fascination. Claudia risked a little smile. Surprisingly, Tahani smiled back, then rose from the low divan and took the brush from Sameera. Pantomiming her own hair being brushed, Tahani spoke a few words to Claudia. Tahani's earnest request was clear. Carefully, Claudia took the brush in her bound hands and motioned for Tahani to sit on the floor in front of her.

Claudia guessed that Tahani was about her own age. But for her dry, coarse skin, she would have been pretty. Her eyes were huge, dark pools which were intensified by her high cheekbones and eyelashes that were enviously long. She was spoiled and bored but unlike Zora, she had the capacity for little flashes of mirth. Claudia had noticed that of the three women, Tahani's character glowed through the layers of cloth and veil; only her eyes flashed with intelligence. Claudia liked Tahani but, understandably, was scared of her, too. She would never relax under the control of strangers.

Now Claudia began to pull the brush through Tahani's thick, black hair. But her bound hands made the task awkward. Boldly, she tapped Tahani on the shoulder and wordlessly explained her dilemma. But Tahani only shook her head and put a finger up to her lips.

Claudia went back to the awkward, two-handed brushing. Tahani's hair was dry and brittle and stroke after stroke could not produce luster. Still, Tahani leaned back against Claudia's legs and Claudia could tell that her captor was drifting into the primal enjoyment of grooming, just as she herself had.

Behind her on the wall, Sameera sat and scowled.

CHAPTER 3

Mr. Bindar stopped the Toyota and rolled down the window. It was late afternoon and the breeze that had blessed them all day was becoming a wind, turning the air into a haze of blowing dirt and sand. As the sun dropped lower and lower, the sky began to turn red, the colors of the desolate rock-strewn landscape all wrong.

Except for the apology Martha had offered, she and Mr. Bindar had not talked since the ugly incident at the well that morning. They had stopped once to drink and to eat dried figs and bread. Even this was done without a word being spoken, and when they had finished, Martha was again glad to disappear behind her veil, to leave the world for the security of soft white cotton.

But with Mr. Bindar's window rolled down, Martha was getting cold and the car was filling with dust. She became a voice again, and albeit a small one, a will. "Mr. Bindar," she said, "please roll the window up now, will you? It's getting nasty in here."

Mr. Bindar did not turn around or acknowledge the request. He continued to drive, staring intensely straight ahead.

Suddenly, Martha knew that something else was wrong. "Mr. Bindar?"

Mr. Bindar glanced over his shoulder at her, and Martha could see that he was perplexed. "Do you smell something?" he asked.

Asking a woman wearing a shroud if she could hear or see or smell anything with acumen was ironic, but Martha let it go. She took a deep breath but all she got was the veil fluttering against her nostrils. "No," she said. "I really can't smell a thing."

Mr. Bindar brought the car to a sudden stop, rolled up the window, and got out. Martha watched him swivel his head around radar-like and sniff the evening air. After a minute or two he was back in the car.

He pointed off to the right, in the direction of low mounds, and said, "They're over there. I would guess hundreds of them."

This mysterious pronouncement swept over Martha in a new wave of dread. She instinctively touched the little silver automatic tucked underneath the abbaya, against her skin, and felt how pathetic it would be against "hundreds of them," against virtually everything that could happen to her in this foreign land.

In the coolest tone she could manage, she said, "Hundreds of whom, please?"

Mr. Bindar turned, the Halloween mask of a face made even more bizarre by the dishabba and, for the first time since she had known him, a wide toothy smile. "Camels. Tuareg camels. Get out of the back seat and undress."

Martha's face froze in shock at Mr. Bindar's order until, under-standing the inappropriateness of her response, Mr. Bindar started to laugh. It was a most amazing, hyena-like outburst, which, even though lunatic, Martha found delightful.

"No," he said, "not undress like you think I mean. Just so you are comfortable. We relax tonight with the Tuareg. They are different. Men wear veils, women don't. They can be very savage warriors, but their enemies are our enemies so tonight we will be friends. I hope."

A few minutes later they were driving towards the ridge, Martha in the front seat, her veil and head covering folded on the back seat. Dressed again in just an abbaya, she felt almost normal. They were off the track now, and the Toyota's wheels spun and slid even more des-perately in the sandy dirt, but it yawed its way along until finally they were at the top of a sandy hill. Below them Martha saw amazing spec-tacle.

A spring pool, surrounded by reeds and date palms, fed a long, nar-row culvert that Martha guessed had been dug centuries earlier and reinforced over time with stones and clay. It ran for fifty yards and along this, standing on both sides, hundreds of camels drank. They were mangy and bad tempered and comical. Some of the camels' humps sagged to one side; virtually all had hairless, peeling patches along their backs and flanks, and plate-size black calluses on their knees. As Martha and Mr. Bindar watched, one of the camels lifted its head and looked around with insolent, bored eyes.

Suddenly, Martha winced as the animal began to make noises that sounded as if it were vomiting and braying at the same time. Now that they were so close, Martha wondered why she hadn't been able to smell the animals, as Mr. Bindar had done, long before.

Closer to the spring, the ground was an immense patchwork of fabulous rugs; the desert floor was covered like a field of wildflowers in reds and blues, swirls and paisleys, greens and oranges, rich arabesques of design. On these carpets baskets and woolen bags and rolled bundles had been piled, and around the perimeter, long, sagging tents, made from some dark, felt-like material, had been erected. In the center, surrounded by carpets, was a bare patch of ground and there a fire was going, kettles suspended over it on ingenious tripods and grates.

The Tuareg were divided into two groups around the fire, women and children on one side, men on the other. Martha estimated about sixty people altogether. Except for the children, every man and woman sat upright, almost at attention, with their legs crossed underneath them. Martha sensed that something, some ritual perhaps, was about to begin. But when the Tuareg saw Martha and Mr. Bindar on top of the ridge, the women began a high-pitched, shrieking ululation, and the men jumped to their feet. Each man reached for the oily black material, part of the headdress which hung down under his chin, and quickly folded it up and over his face. And then each man produced a long, curved dagger from his belt. Martha shuddered. The Tuareg men formed a terrifying wedge between the intruders and the women, who had continued their fabulous wail.

Mr. Bindar took Martha's arm and awkwardly they made their way towards the camp, kicking and lunging through the sand and dirt. As they approached, the women's wailing died down and by the time they were within thirty feet of the perimeter of carpets, all that Martha could hear was the fire snapping, an occasional camel snort, and the tents flapping against the wind.

The phalanx of Tuareg warriors stood directly in front of them. Mr. Bindar positioned Martha behind him. "Look down at the ground I speak to them," he instructed.

Martha was both anxious to make amends to Mr. Bindar and grateful for his protection from these frightening men. "Believe me," she said in a tone that belied her nervousness, "I will be happy to do anything you ask."

Martha was acutely aware of dark eyes glaring out from the folds of material, and of the voices that sounded more like song than speech. She watched Mr. Bindar speak to a Tuareg who came to stand in front of the other men. He looked particularly aristocratic and, to Martha, about ten feet tall. Mr. Bindar made a short bow and salaam, gestured back to her, and then put his hands to his mouth, pantomiming the act of eating.

And just like that the tension broke. The Tuareg man Mr. Bindar had been talking to put his dagger back in his belt, brushed hands with Mr. Bindar, and walked back to the fire with the others.

"They speak mostly Tamershak so I don't understand much," Mr. Bindar said breathlessly when he'd trudged back up the sandy slope to where Martha stood. "But they welcome us to share the well at El Fal. I am going to get the car and you should now go sit with the women. They will be very curious so don't be alarmed when they touch you."

Martha saw the Tuareg women looking at her and instinctively, self-consciously, she licked her lips and ran her hands over her hair, before laughing at herself for her absurd, out-of-place gestures. Slowly, she walked down to the women. Almost as one they stood and began to shout to each other in a high, excited, rapid syllables. Martha was surrounded. She assumed the women were trying to figure out from what exotic tribe from the south this tall, dark woman hailed. Hands pinched her hair, groped at her breasts, even pulled at her lips to expose her teeth. The women looked at her ankles, each wrist, each finger, pulled up the hem of her abbaya so they could look up underneath. Their hands touched and poked; their painful shrieks of surprise and discovery began to suffocate Martha. She felt her mood morph from amusement to tolerance to endurance. Just before her mood shifted to panic, the group opened up and led Martha to the fire where, by gesture, she was invited to sit. The half circle of women formed on either side of her, and, just as Martha had seen them from the top of the ridge, they sat upright and very still, staring at the palm fronds burning in the fire and at the men sitting on the other side, their faces wrapped in oily folds.

The women didn't look Arabic. They were very dark but Martha could tell they were not African, either. Most of them wore black, muslin robes and over this they had wrapped a decorative, embroidered shawl, also black, which covered their shoulders and, for some of the women, their heads. They all wore silver and brass jewelry, some of it around the forehead, some in layers of heavy necklaces or bracelets or large hoop earrings.

One woman, a servant maybe, went to work at the fire. A few moments later she handed Martha a tin plate of food: pieces of chicken, flat bread, a little pile of dates. Then, one woman rose from her position in the circle, walked over to Martha, and solemnly dropped a necklace of brass beads the size of giant pearls over her head. Without once having looked directly at her, the woman resumed her place by the fire and then another rose, and again without making eye contact, put a silver ring on Martha's thumb. Another brought her a stack of silver bracelets, fitting one after the other over Martha's hands. Another woman brought a small woven bag of glass beads; another, a small bag of what looked liked scorpion stingers. The women watched the presentations, nodding to each other with pleasure. Shortly, the gift giving stopped and the servant woman disappeared from her place by the fire. Martha watched the Tuareg men drink tea, bringing the little glasses up underneath their veils.

Soon the Toyota came into view; Mr. Bindar parked just outside the circle of rugs. Martha watched as he got out of the car and walked over to the men. He was carrying the guns he had taken off the nomads' donkeys earlier that day. The Yuareg men rose, took the proffered guns and sighted along the barrels. They passed them around, from man to man, and after each had handled a gun, each brushed hands with Mr. Bindar. Finally, the men once again took their positions by the fire.

It was darker now, almost night. The men and women had grown silent and motionless again. The children seemed to have disappeared. The fire snapped, sending little sparks up into the air; somewhere out in the darkness a bird called and once or twice a camel bawled. And then, the women sitting around Martha began to sway back and forth, first one, then another, until all were swaying in unison.

From the men's side of the fire rose the sound of a flute, and then a falsetto voice, and then another and another joined it, each in atonal counterpoint, wailing into the night. The tempo became faster and faster and the women swayed with the men's song, their hands dancing in the air before them. Martha sensed that the women were being serenaded. Through unflagging repetition the men's song became more frenzied, excited, sexual.

And then one of the Tuareg warriors stood and began to twirl. Another joined him, and another, until six men were spinning, arms outstretched, their cloaks billowing around them, their dark eyes flashing on and off, on and off, as they spun past the fire.

Martha watched the ring of dancing, turbaned men and the women who were exciting this display. All seemed entranced by the pure vitality of the ceremony. Martha looked up at the stars and thought of a fireworks display. But these bursts did not fade; they remained brilliant, sparkling, indelible explosions in the dome of the Sahara sky. And she thought, "Life is just this simple, just this wonderful. God, how we ruin it."

And then Martha felt the brass necklace gently slapping against her chest as she, too, began to sway to the men's song, and she thought she could feel the soft inside of Claudia's thighs.

CHAPTER 4

Claudia awoke and, climbing down from the platform bed, bathed. As she did every morning, a servant unlocked the door to bring her a tray of coffee, always too strong but better than the sweet tea the women seemed to drink by the gallons, and her usual breakfast of orange slices and sweetened bread. She put the silver tray down on a small table against a wall.

Most mornings the servant then made Claudia's bed. First, she gathered the muslin curtains to the bed's four posts and tied them in place. Next, she unfolded the heavy brocade spread and smoothed it out, folding it perfectly over the three pillows fluffed and lined up at the top. Then she opened the long lace curtains so the light slanting through the latticed windows was less filtered. Finally, as if all had been prelude, she delicately spread out the abayya Claudia was to wear that day so it looked like a beautiful, pleated scallop.

But this morning there was only the delivery of the silver tray. Claudia sat on the edge of the bed, holding a giant towel around her, and watched as the servant left, locking the door her with a click. She didn't walk over to the little dressing table against the wall, as she did every morning, to brush her hair and use the little jars of makeup that had been left for her, hoping that one of them might be useful against the dryness that was beginning to chafe her once soft skin. Something was different.

The collar that was buckled on her every morning hung from a wooden peg over the head of the bed. Claudia always dreaded the collar being fastened, but this morning, having been given no clothes, she felt even more vulnerable than usual. She dreaded more than ever the door opening and the humiliation of the collar being fastened around her neck and the shame of her hands being bound by the yards of ribbon. And so she sat staring at the door, holding the towel tightly in place.

She didn't have to wait for long. The door opened and Sameera came in carrying a bundle. Claudia assumed it was her clothes for the day, but when Sameera put the bundle on the bed, Claudia saw that on top of the bundle sat a coil of rope and a big square of a folded Hermes scarf. She instinctively knew what this meant and fought the impulse to knock Sameera over and run.

Days of controlling Claudia had emboldened Sameera. With her confidence in Claudia's submission had come a growing sexual familiarity that expressed itself, sometimes obscenely, sometimes as pouting meanness. Claudia wanted to encourage the part of the girl's infatuation that she hoped she could manipulate. She wanted somehow to keep Sameera enchanted, not frustrated. But each day it was harder and harder for Claudia to be civil to the spoiled, willful teenager.

After laying the bundle on the bed, Sameera placed the silver breakfast tray in the bathroom and then sat on the floor in front of Claudia as she often did, as if in supplication, to massage her feet. But this morning Claudia pulled her feet away; she didn't want to make whatever was to come next any easier for Sameera. Claudia had learned that Sameera tied knots as tightly as anyone else but that she also needed to be forgiven by her prisoner, morning after morning, for doing so. With a sinking heart, Claudia had begun to see the subtle but unmistakable flicker of power and the satisfaction of ownership in Sameera's eyes when the buckle was being fastened or the knots being tied.

Claudia stood and looked down at Sameera. In a tone that betrayed both her anger and her fear, she said, "What are you going to do to me?"

Sameera looked up at Claudia, then down again to the floor. "We want to take you outside, to show you the souk. We thought you would enjoy that. Tahani likes you. She gets your cello for you today to keep in your room. She wants you to go with us." Then, in a voice that was barely audible, she added, "I always like you. You are so beautiful. I like to take care of you."

Yes, Claudia thought, *like a pony. And I don't believe a word of what you say about giving me back my beloved cello.*

"If you like me," Claudia said in a voice of forced gentleness, "you won't tie me every morning. I have no place to go. I won't run away. I don't even know where I am. If you like me you should help me." Claudia leaned down, tenderly took Sameera's head in her hands, and looked directly into the girl's eyes. "Please," she said, "won't you help me?"

Sameera pulled away from Claudia and stood, now the petulant child who wasn't getting her way. "Zora tells me to do this. She is very mean. She will be mean to me if I don't. I must get you ready to go outside now or Zora will come in and beat you and me. You know how mean she is."

Claudia knew. And Claudia also knew how much comfort Sameera took in having the resource of a bully to enforce her will. Yet Sameera seemed to be the only weak link in her chain of keepers and Claudia silently vowed to continue to work on her later.

Sameera took the rope from the bed and, with more hesitation than assertion, asked Claudia to put her wrists together. Claudia held her hands out in front of her and, hiding her loathing, asked sweetly that they not be tied too tightly. "Yesterday my hands were quite uncomfortable," she said. "And the rope will hurt even more than the ribbons."

"No," Sameera replied. "You must have them behind you this morning. Zora says so. So does Tahani."

Claudia hadn't been tied this way since she had been kidnapped and taken to whatever version of hell this was. Remembering how uncomfortable and helpless she had felt scared her. "No, Sameera," she said. There was not a bit of patronization in her voice. She was deadly earnest in her plea. "Tie my hands in front, please. Zora won't care if she sees you have done a good job."

"Zora will care. Don't make me call her," Sameera said in a tone that just barely dared to threaten. Then she walked behind Claudia, reached around, and tentatively took one hand, then the other, and crossed them behind Claudia's back. The towel that Claudia had been barely holding in place by squeezing her arms against her body fell to the floor.

Naked, Claudia looked over her shoulder at the girl. "Please," she said, "not this way, Sameera." But the girl's only response was the first loop of rope, pulled so tightly around both wrists that Claudia winced. Even Zora could not have made it hurt more. The rope went around and around, each circuit ending with a sharp tug, and then she could feel Sameera strain at making the first knot as tight as possible. Claudia despaired of finding a way to stop the ignominy of what was being done to her.

Sameera finished her nasty job. When she spoke again, all the sweetness had come back into her voice. She was again the poor innocent girl who was being made to do bad things. "I am so sorry," she purred. "Please go sit at your little table. I will make you comfortable today. I will take care of you."

"You don't take care of me at all, Sameera," Claudia replied boldly. "You hurt me. We could be special friends."

"Ssssh. You are being very bad to me this morning. I am trying hard to be your friend but you don't care. Now, go sit so I can tie a pretty scarf around your mouth. You get gagged before you can go outside."

Claudia heard an unmistakable but self-conscious thrill in Sameera's bad French. She no longer had any idea of how to negotiate with this child, this sadistic hoyden. She felt dread and deep shame for what was about to be done to her, as if she had let herself down, as if she had missed something she could have done to save herself. Worse, she felt she was on the edge of pleading with Sameera, and the thought sickened her. It would have been better if Zora were her tormentor; at least Claudia would know she was physically outmatched. Acquiesce to this mere girl was humiliating.

With as much dignity as she could muster, naked and bound the way she was, Claudia walked over to the little table as she had been told. In the mirror she watched Sameera unfold the gaily-colored Hermes scarf and hold it out in front of her like a small, shimmering curtain. Next, Sameera placed the scarf over her own face and stroked the silk gently, seductively.

Claudia was afraid to look away. She wanted to be prepared for whatever strange thing was to come next.

Now Sameera gathered the scarf against her cheek, like a child holding a favorite blanket. "Isn't it beautiful?" she said. "I select it just for you. It will be pretty on you." Claudia watched as the girl folded the scarf and held it against her own mouth in imitation of a gag. Her eyes sparkled with excitement.

Claudia felt herself tense, felt the last bit of her composure wane. Sameera now stood just behind her. Slowly, she brushed the folded scarf across Claudia's face once, twice, and then opening it, draped it over Claudia's head. The scarf fell to Claudia's collarbone, completely obscuring her face.

Claudia sensed the girl circle her. She felt her run a finger lightly over the silk that covered her face—swirls against Claudia's cheeks, her chin, her eyelids, her lips. Sameera blew against the silk; it fluttered against Claudia's face and tickled uncomfortably.

"See how pretty I can make you feel?" The voice was a whisper. Claudia tried to see her tormentor through the thick, soft silk, but it was impossible. Part of her wanted to anticipate Sameera's next touch and turn away from it. But rather than play the girl's sick game she sat deathly still and endured Sameera's provocations.

Claudia felt Sameera's tongue in her ear; she felt her at her back again. She felt Sameera's hand lift her chin, felt her lips kiss her hair through the draped scarf. Still, Claudia sat rigidly; she refused to offer this girl any sort of response.

"Guess where I touch you next?" Sameera purred. And then her hand clamped over Claudia's mouth, forcing her head back. With her other hand Sameera twirled Claudia's bare nipple. Instinct made Claudia try to twist her head free but Sameera held her tight. Bound and blinded, Claudia felt the silk of the scarf drawn up into her nostrils as she breathed in, felt it puff out when she exhaled. She couldn't help but cry out; the hand over her mouth was too tight and her plea for mercy was nothing more than a strangled grunt.

Sameera gently pulled Claudia's nipples, kneaded and massaged each breast. "It feels good, no?" she whispered.

Again, all Claudia could do was moan her protest.

Sameera abruptly took her hands off of Claudia's mouth and breasts. Claudia heard the girl walk away, felt the girl's petulance. She heard one of the little drawers in the dark, cracked chest across the room open. And then there was the tinkle of a chain, and Sameera was back. She jerked the little bench on which Claudia sat away from the table and kneeled at Claudia's feet. Instinctively, Claudia looked down to watch what was happening but the scarf still blinded her. She felt Sameera attach one end of the chain to her jeweled anklet, thread it onto another fetter, and lock it onto the other ankle. Claudia fervently hoped the chain between her ankles was long enough so that she could walk with some shred of dignity.

Sameera stood up, her silence angry and pouting. She slid the scarf off Claudia's head, and carefully, almost lovingly, folded it into a long rectangle. Then, she tied a large, elaborate knot right in the middle. Claudia felt sick.

"I am going to gag you now," the girl said. "Do you want a drink of water first? I keep you gagged for a long time today. Maybe you should be gagged every day until you learn to be nicer."

Claudia still hoped, however weakly, that there might be an opportunity to turn Sameera's perverse adoration to her advantage. "Yes," she replied. "Some water please, Sameera."

Sameera went to the chest across the room and returned with a tray on which sat a zinc pitcher and glasses. She poured water into one of the glasses and held it to Claudia's mouth while she drank. Claudia asked for a second glass, and when she finished that, Sameera used the sleeve of her abayya to dab at the water that had dribbled onto Claudia's chin.

Sameera put the glass back on the tray, picked up the scarf, and walked behind Claudia. Again, Claudia watched her captor in the mirror and saw animation return to Sameera's face.

"Do you know how much that hurts the corners of my mouth?" Claudia said softly. "Please, if you need to put on the gag, please not so tight. Please Sameera."

"Sssh," the girl hissed. "I'm tired of you."

Claudia watched as Sameera stretched the scarf in front of her face. She watched as Sameera placed the knot against her mouth and waited for Claudia to open it. For a moment there was an impasse. Claudia stared directly into the girl's eyes in the mirror. Sameera stared back. Claudia opened her mouth to plea once more but the knot was in and the scarf pulled so tight that tears sprung to her eyes.

Sameera patted her captive on the cheek. Then she came around and straddled Claudia. Grabbing the ends of the scarf in one hand she yanked Claudia's head backwards, so that she was helplessly looking up into Sameera's face.

"I wanted to pleasure you this morning," the girl said, almost cooing, "but you were very bad. Some night I tie you to your bed so I can, yes?" And then, to Claudia's horror, the girl kissed her as if trying to force her tongue right past the gag into Claudia's mouth.

CHAPTER 5

"The Tuareg know Djanet," Mr. Bindar told Martha. "They can help us get Miss Simmerhorn out of Algeria. If we find her."

Martha and Mr. Bindar had been awakened by the angry grunts of camels being loaded, then forced to unlock their seemingly arthritic knees and rise, back end to front end. That the Tuareg could decamp so fast was a wonder. It was hard to look at the rocks and the dirt and the scrawny acacia trees, and imagine that the life and color of the night before would soon be gone without a trace.

In the light of morning no one paid the least bit of attention to Martha and Mr. Bindar. When the last cumbersome bundles and floppy rolls of rugs were tied in place, the Tuareg men climbed onto their camels, perched in precarious comfort twenty feet above the ground. The women took their place in a group behind the men, wrapped against the wind and wind-blown sand, and the children ran in and out among them, eager to begin the day's journey, another in the largely unbroken cycle of moving on. Once the Tuareg had started on their way, no one looked back except for a bare-footed, shabby boy whose job it was to direct their goats forward with a stick. The boy looked over his shoulder and stuck out his tongue at Martha and Mr. Bindar as if to say, " Ha, ha. You can't go with us."

Martha was tired. The dancing of the night before had gone on for hours, and it wasn't until some of the Tuareg men had dropped from sheer exhaustion that the circle had started to break apart. The sparks from the fire slowly had died and quietly, the Tuareg had disappeared into the low, dark tents.

Mr. Bindar and Martha had slept on cots by the Toyota, and now, the Tuareg gone, they packed their own belongings in relative silence.

According to Mr. Bindar they would be in Djanet by the early afternoon.

Before leaving, Mr. Bindar put on a djellaba, a long-sleeve hooded robe that hung almost to the ground. Martha watched him tuck the Uzi and three extra clips in a belt before putting the robe over his head. She wondered how he could get at them in a hurry but didn't ask. She had seen Mr. Bindar do several seemingly impossible things.

As she had been told to do, Martha put on the immense drape of a haik, the hem of which fell to her ankles. The niqab went over the bridge of her nose so that it fell around the lower half of her face and down across her breasts. The head covering obscured Martha's forehead, and wrapped around the front of her shoulders. Finally, like a frightened turtle withdrawing into its shell, Martha drew her hands up inside the haik's huge sleeves. The last bit of her physical self disappeared.

Again, covered so thoroughly against the eyes of the world, Martha felt safe. Underneath the coverings, she still wore the brass necklace, the ring on her thumb, the layers of silver bracelets. Underneath, she still carried her little automatic in its cloth holster and belt. Underneath, she was still Martha Bekele.

Martha climbed into the back seat of the Toyota and watched as Mr. Bindar screwed a silencer on to a huge pistol he produced from an oily box underneath the front seat. He then retrieved his prayer rug from the trunk and put it next to him on the front seat before sliding the pistol inside its folds.

The Toyota slid and spun its way back up to the track. Once on course, heading south, Mr. Bindar looked at Martha in the rear view and began to talk.

"The Tuareg say there are two palaces where your friend could be. Both huge and behind walls. They don't go near them, too many guards. All our national soldiers have left town, gone somewhere on the border with Libya, so Prince Jed al Hann rules like a little king. The Tuareg say that he is a fanatic and that his guards are moral police. They patrol the city and beat or maim people who are not dressed or acting like good Muslims. A terrible place for infidels like us, no?"

Martha saw Mr. Bindar smile as he said this and she felt a rush of affection for him and his attempt to break the tension. But now, possibly just hours away from a reunion Claudia, she couldn't stop the desperation, suppressed so well for days, from returning. She tried not to think about how Claudia was being treated or about in what condition they might find her. She tried not to think about how they were going to get her out of the prince's palace once they did find her. Mostly, Martha tried not to think about the awful possibility that she and Mr. Bindar might never find Claudia.

Martha remembered the captive woman on the ship—the one who had looked up at her with desperate, pleading eyes—and tried not to think about the long odds of a happy ending to her own tortuous story.

"Mr. Bindar," she said, "if there are soldiers on the border, how can we get into Libya ourselves? Your government wants Prince Jed al Hann as an ally so won't they act on his behalf and stop us?"

Mr. Bindar laughed. "Of course not," he said. "We must not get caught by Jed al Hann's police but the army won't help catch us. The prince is their enemy and it doesn't matter who tells them otherwise. An enemy of their enemy is their friend. Besides, the Tuareg go back and forth, wander across conflict and borders like dust. They know how to be invisible by riding on camels in caravans a mile long or jamming themselves onto trucks like piles of fruit."

Martha felt a small ray of hope. "So," she said, "what happens if we do get into Libya?"

"Good for you," Mr. Bindar replied promptly, "bad for me. I won't go. They would kill me, say I am a spy. I'll send you and Miss Simmerhorn across the border with the Tuareg and I'll go back to Algiers. Libya will use you as proof of our treachery and then they will return you for favors from your country."

Martha pondered this information before asking, "Mr. Bindar, why are you helping us? If Jed al Hann is no longer an enemy of your government, aren't you risking trouble for yourself and embarrassment for Algeria?"

Mr. Bindar spoke as if he were carefully choosing his words. "Yesterday," he said, "Jed al Hann was our enemy. Today he is our friend. Tomorrow he will be our enemy again. Every day we try different combinations for peace. The FLN, the Islamic Salvation Front, the Armed Islamic Group, our death squads, the Groupe Islamic Armee, the Islamic Salvation Front. We need to read the newspapers every day to see who is playing on our side and who is playing against us. Our version of your sports page."

Martha smiled; for a moment she forgot that because of her veil Mr. Bindar could not see her mouth.

Mr. Bindar went on. The more he explained, the more angry his voice became. "All the while we try hard to act like a civilized country in the eyes of the rest of the world. And civilized countries do not allow Americans to be kidnapped and terrorists like Nikkos Lindos to throw young women into the sea for having love. Today or tomorrow," he vowed, "I will kill Nikkos Lindos and it does not matter whose side he is on."

Since leaving the town of Mohammadia days before, their track had been level across stony dirt, only occasionally broken by low ridges, piles of sharp rocks, spikes of acacia, and tufts of brittle grass. But in the last hour the landscape had begun to change. To Martha, the unbroken landscape of sand brought a feeling of deep desolation.

Dunes rose around them, inexorably slow sand tides, in places forming hurricane-sized waves. The crests of these waves seemed to smoke as wind blew sand from them hundreds of grains at a time, creating patterns on the troughs of the waves.

The world was soft. Nothing sharp remained, every straight line had meandered, every sharp edge had been rounded off. The world was a smothering, shifting softness.

Martha leaned closer to the window and pulled her veil down a little off her nose so that she could see the bizarre landscape more clearly.

"This is part of a Great Erg," Mr. Bindar explained. "It goes all the way into Libya. In fact, we fight them for it, pretty stupid, huh? For sure it's a bad place to run out of water. Wells and villages are buried out here and then the sand shifts, ten, twenty years later, and the villages are uncovered and people move back in. In the meantime other villages drown. First the sand comes underneath their doors and they try, week after week, to sweep it away. And then they give up, sometimes waiting until the sand is two, three feet deep in their rooms, and move, knowing that some day some one in their family in some future generation will move back in."

Martha thought with wonder about the people who clung to their home in spite of sure disaster the next day or the next year. Land, she thought, was as solid as love.

"My government built a highway across," Mr. Bindar went on. "It was buried before they even finished. So then they went back and put cement posts up to show where the highway used to be and now the posts are buried, too. Someday when you come back the sand will be someplace else and there will be a highway here with nice posts all along the side. But the next time you come back after that, it will be gone again." Mr. Bindar paused, as if for effect. "The Tuareg use the stars to cross. They say that someday the sand will cover them, too."

Again, Martha felt genuine warmth for Mr. Bindar, this man who was risking so much for her and for Claudia. She resisted the impulse to touch him, as she might have touched a helpful colleague in her office ten stories above Montgomery Street in San Francisco, a lifetime ago. But then she leaned forward and gently put her hand on his shoulder.

"How do you know where you're going?" she asked.

"Me?" he said. "I have no idea. I've been lost for days." And then he laughed his delightful hyena laugh and showed her the compass that was in his hand.

CHAPTER 6

Prince Jed al Hann had given Nikkos a hero's reception upon his return. Not only had Nikkos restored the honor of the prince's family by dispatching the prince's disrespectful daughter, he had further embellished the prince's nobility by returning with a hostage taken from the very country responsible for his family's disgrace.

The prince's satisfaction was immense, and he had no intent to return the American. It was a simple exchange between countries. You took my daughter so I take one of yours.

Still, Prince Jed al Hann had no idea what to do with his captive. But since she was a replacement for his daughter, she was his responsibility, now involved in his honor, and he was responsible for her conduct. Keeping her safe and chaste in his harem with his daughters, Sameera and Zora, and his wife, Tahani, seemed like the right thing to do. They would teach this American the loyalty and obedience he expected from the women in his family.

But Nikkos felt differently. His victorious return was soured when Claudia fell immediately under the prince's protection and Nikkos was forbidden ever to see her again. That Claudia should have been given to *him* seemed only fair. That she should be protected from him was an insult. She, a whore from the decadent breeder of whores, America, was too good for Nikkos, the Mahdi? So the banquet given to him in his honor, the emerald ring, the rhinoceros-horn dagger—without the real prize these were insults, too.

He decided to go to Libya, a country that understood terrorism and would respect his talents, and then Prince Jed al Hann would see what kind of an enemy he had made. But before he left, he would spoil the prince's American prize, show that not even the sanctity of the royal harem was off limits to the scourge of the Mahdi.

For a bribe of hashish, Zora, that pig, would help him. For hashish, Zora would do anything.

CHAPTER 7

The chain linking her ankles together was just long to allow Claudia to walk in mincing steps. The journey from her room to the tiled porch of the palace seemed interminable. And then, it was almost over.

Even though she was engulfed in a haik and a head covering which hung down her back to her waist; even though her face was covered by the niqab that hung down from the bridge of her nose; even though her wrists and the corners of her mouth already ached; and even though she was worried about Sameera's progressively violent and demeaning behavior, when the first and then the second great door had been unlocked by guards and Claudia stood in the bright morning sun, she felt more hopeful than she had since being taken off the Swan II against her will. How long ago was that, she wondered? Two weeks, maybe three weeks. She didn't know.

While the women stood on the tiled porch and waited for their ride, Claudia try to note as much as she could of her surroundings, and to burn the memories into her brain, all without calling attention to her endeavors. She could see that the palace was on the ridge of a hill and that the town, just below, was terraced into slopes on both sides of a lush valley of date palms. On the other side of a low wall several yards in front of them was what must have been the center of a very old town. Its narrow streets twisted crazily between high, pink stone buildings and most of the flat roofs had been made into patios, furnished with potted plants and cushions and rugs. Claudia counted at least seven pencil-like minarets and wondered which imams—by this time she had learned to recognize the personal calls of at least four—belonged to which minaret. From below she could hear a dog bark, a muffler-less truck, and the static of record-played-backwards radio music.

In spite of the veil that covered the lower half of her face and fluttered against her mouth and nose when she took a deep breath, Claudia could smell fresh air, air without a trace of the heavy incense that burned day and night in the oda. She breathed in as deeply as she could and sighed behind the gag.

A Lincoln limousine pulled up the long curved drive and stopped alongside the porch. The driver got out, careful not to look at the women, and opened the back door of the car. Tahani nudged Claudia forward, as if she were inviting, not forcing, her to go for a ride. Claudia shuffled forward but her chained ankles prevented her from stepping up and inside the car.

She heard Zora's coarse laugh behind her, and felt hands on her arms. It was Tahani. She turned Claudia around and helped her sit into the car first and then lift both her feet in. Because of the slippery leather seats, Claudia had difficulty sitting upright without sliding forward or to the side. Finally, she was able to establish some kind of balance by leaning against one of the doors. Zora squatted across from her on the jump seat; Sameera and Tahani slipped in next to Claudia.

The Lincoln pulled out of the drive. Claudia stared out the window, interested in the diversion of new scenery and instinctively trying to memorize the landscape of flight. Unfortunately, this time her concentrated interest was obvious. Sameera pulled Claudia against her shoulder, and mocking the affectionate gesture of a lover, put an arm around her and covered Claudia's eyes with her soft hand.

Claudia sat as still and unmoving as the movement of the car allowed. Here was yet another example of how Sameera's crush was fast becoming a violent infatuation. Claudia remembered what Sameera had said a few hours ago, about tying her down and 'loving' her, about raping her. More than anything Claudia wanted to try one more time to test the ropes that bound her, but she knew that cuddled so close to Sameera like a submissive lover, she wouldn't get far.

The ride lasted about ten minutes. When the car stopped, and when Sameera took her hand from Claudia's eyes, she saw a broad dusty square surrounded by a low mud-brick wall and plain trees which formed the broad perimeter of an outdoor market. It was as if everything edible within hundreds of miles had been brought to this square and proudly displayed. On the ground were huge piles of nuts, grains, dates, oranges, figs, fifty kilo bags of Indian rice, pomegranates, bundles of sticks, and unrecognizable husks and leaves and shavings. Consumers, all men, milled around these offerings and past makeshift pens containing sheep and goats, their bawling lost in the din of the loud bargaining going on around them. Next to the low mud wall, two young camels chewed their cud, indifferent to the flies that buzzed in clouds around their heads.

To Claudia, the crowd was an unidentifiable mixture or tribes and races. Some men were dressed in turbans or wrapped in voluminous headdresses or hoods or ghutras; others were bare headed. Some men wore elaborate robes or burnooses or long vests or cloaks fastened at the neck; others were almost loincloth naked.

The four women got out of the Lincoln. Tahani, Zora, and Sameera herded Claudia around the walled perimeter of the square, a bright white flock of four veiled women moving past the haggling men unnoticed, ignored. They walked up a little street between mud walls that rose too high for Claudia to see over, and then around a sharp corner. They passed through a dark arcade; it was then that Claudia felt if they had stepped off the edge of the coherent earth. She found herself in a labyrinth of narrow, camel-wide lanes that twisted and branched, doubled back, came to blind ends, or descended in steep steps to another level. Claudia felt horribly disoriented. She was sure she'd never be able to find her way out of this dim, vast, warren of cells and low, dark doorways and stalls.

The women had entered the souk. Lining the network of alleys, buildings made of mud and stone rose three, sometimes four windowless stories. Hands reached out of dark doorways, proffering a swath of material, amber jewelry, little vials of perfume, transistor radios, candied dates, tea in little zinc cups, strange leather pouches. Shopkeepers, ghostly robed figures, appeared in doorways and beckoned with imploring tones for the women them to follow them inside, moaning when the women walked on. From each threshold came uniquely pungent incense and high, tinny music. The smells and the sounds, the twisting, dark confusion of the souk affected Claudia like a drug. She felt the place was both demented and wonderful.

After days, weeks of being confined in the oda, Claudia's mind reeled. She felt slightly dizzy and tried to focus on her feet, willing herself not to stumble as she would certainly fall flat on her face. Each mincing step on the uneven stone pavement was tentative, made more difficult by her inability to look down and see past the niqab or the fullness of the haik that hung to the ground. Inevitably, she did stumble a few times, causing Zora to laugh loudly. Mercifully, Sameera and Tahani were there to grab her before she fell.

Finally, the women came around a sharp corner, one of countless sharp corners. In a dark doorway stood three women looking down at a little monkey scratching itself with a turnip. The women were mirror images of Claudia and her captors, veiled by yards of fine cotton, and shrouded beyond any recognizable form. To Claudia, each woman seemed to lack a personal identity.

She was surprised then when one by one the women in the doorway shrieked and giggled and extended their hands from the depths of their robes to reach for Tahani, Zora, and Sameera. Claudia's captors responded with equal enthusiasm while she stood still and alone.

A man, perhaps the monkey's owner, suddenly appeared as if from nowhere, clearly seeing an opportunity for profit. He held aside the heavy curtain that served as a door and beckoned the women into what Claudia assumed was some sort of shop. They ducked through the low doorway and once inside, Claudia saw that they were in a series of bar,e mud brick cells, one connected to another by other low doorways, each cell barely illuminated by a single light bulb which hung down from the wooden ceiling on a cord. The man yelled an order and clapped his hands and two small, barefooted boys appeared from the gloom within. Together, the boys dragged a rug from another cell and spread it on the floor. They ran off and a moment later returned dragging cushions, then wooden benches, and finally, a round low table that they placed in the middle of the rug and set with seven small tin glasses. The bare room had been converted into a little tea parlor.

The proprietor, after being assured that the room was arranged to his liking, left and returned shortly, struggling with a wooden, latticed screen which he unfolded and positioned in such a way that the women would be assured a private teatime, that hijab, as Claudia understood it, would be honored.

Finally, the proprietor sent the boys away with a shout and the monkey with a kick and then bowing obsequies, disappeared himself.

The women had been silent during the preparations, but as soon as the proprietor disappeared behind the screen, they resumed their excited chatter and giggling. Zora roughly placed Claudia on one of the benches and rejoined the other women. Claudia sat she stiffly, immobile and silent, watching. She wondered if her presence in the palace of the prince was a secret and, if so, if there might be a way of turning this unexpected tea party into an opportunity for rescue. Very slowly and very carefully, Claudia shifted in an attempt to make the haik ride up off her slippers a little and expose, just barely, her chained ankles. After a moment or two, Claudia leaned back against the mud brick wall and slowly, slowly stretched her legs until she could easily see the jeweled fetter, the plain cuff, and the chrome chain linking the two. And, of course, the sores and bruises they had caused.

It wasn't long before Claudia discovered that she wasn't a dirty little secret but a celebrity and that no one in this little cell was the least bit interested in rescuing her and her damaged ankles.

Roughly, Zora returned and grabbed Claudia by the arm, forcing her to stand. The women's excited chattering stopped and three new pairs of dark eyes stared at her through slits in sheaths of white as Claudia took humiliating little steps towards them.

"Our friends want to meet you," Sameera said. And then she began to remove Claudia's head covering, reaching up to carefully lift it off her forehead and then folding it back until it draped across her shoulders like an oversized shawl. Next she slid the niqab down off Claudia's nose, worked it past the gag, until it gathered around her neck like a bib.

Claudia looked at the three unknown women, tried with her eyes to assert some dignity, but their hands were all over her. They petted her hair; they stroked the Hermes gag and pushed curiously on the knot. One lifted strands of Claudia's hair to see how long it was; another felt the smoothness of her cheek. And all the while they chattered excitedly.

The few remaining shreds of Claudia's dignity abandoned her. She lowered her eyes, ashamed.

But her humiliation was to get worse. The next stop on Sameera's proud tour of Claudia's body required lifting the hem of Claudia's haik. First, she lifted it from the back so that the women could see the rope that bound Claudia's hands. Sameera grabbed Claudia's wrists and roughly pulled them up, away her body. Claudia was thrust forward. The women's giggling seared through her like a hot knife. Satisfied with her prisoner's performance, Sameera released Claudia's hands and dropped the hem of the haik.

Claudia's heart sank yet again. Why didn't Tahani stop this abusive show? Was her indifference that embedded?

Sameera knelt on the floor and grabbed the front hem of Claudia's haik. Claudia looked down at the girl and shook her head. A gurgle of protest burst from her throat; the women found this lame attempt at resistance particularly amusing and shrieked with laughter. Grinning, Sameera lifted the front of the haik and then pulled it right over Claudia's head, effectively shrouding her in a giant hood.

Claudia was more humiliated than she had ever been in all her life. Still, a part of her was glad to be covered, glad to disappear, glad not to have to look into the eyes of the people who were treating her so disgustingly.

The women fell silent. Claudia felt a hand rub against her stomach, and another feel the firmness of her breasts. She shivered at this rude probing but was helpless to escape as Zora's rough hands held her tightly from behind. Now another hand began to slide down her stomach toward the cleft between her legs. It was Sameera's, she was sure, and she prepared for the worst. And then, suddenly, Claudia felt the hand slapped away and Tahani's voice, admonishing and angry. Claudia sensed someone else now directly in front of her. And then Tahini was lifting the material over and off Claudia's head and, as if she were drawing the curtain on a lewd act, she lowered the haik over Claudia's naked, bound body. The irony of such protection did not escape Claudia.

The audience was awkwardly quiet. Claudia gave Tahani a look of absolute gratitude, and Tahani returned it with one of embarrassed apology. She led Claudia back to the bench against the wall and helped her to sit, as far away from the rest of the women as the little room allowed.

Tea was then served on a brass tray that was slid around the side of the screen. The women drank by lifting the little glasses up underneath their veils, as if sneaking sips. Sameera offered to remove Claudia's gag so she could have a glass, but Claudia shook her head. The idea of Sameera's touching her again was as repugnant as the taste of the sticky sweet tea.

No one looked at Claudia again until the tea party ended. With formality the women hugged each other and then each of the three women who had been strangers to Claudia came over to where she sat and hugged her, too. Claudia tensed; it took her a moment to realize that the women were not hugging her not with ridicule but with genuine, solemn warmth. Then their hands disappeared inside their haiks and one by one the women glided like wraiths around the interior screen and were gone.

Zora pulled Claudia to her feet. Sameera secured the niquab over the bridge of Claudia's nose so it covered the lower half of her face.

Then she lifted the head covering off Claudia's shoulders and placed it over the top of her head, folding it down on her forehead.

Tahani put a few coins on the brass tray and they left, the proprietor salaaming to them from the doorway.

Claudia was surprised at how quickly they were out again in the sun.

The women stopped by a two-foot high concrete wall that formed the border of a grove of huge date palms. Channels for water had been dug into the sandy earth between the trees and around these channels several dark men were working, raking them clear of the fronds and fallen dates which threatened to clog the trickle of water.

Claudia's captors sat on the wall; Claudia hoped the excursion was coming to an end and that they were waiting for the ride back to the palace. She watched what traffic there was with little interest: an occasional filthy bus; a few trucks back firing between gears; donkeys and Russian Ladas; a smelly diesel Pugeot station wagon maneuvering around a herd of sheep; a motorbike with three boys balanced on it; a nearly naked man pushing a cart.

Claudia was startled by Sameera's mouth at her ear. "Remember," she whispered through the veil, "tomorrow night I tie you and love you."

Panic swept through Claudia for what seemed like the millionth time that day. But suddenly, her attention was caught by the incredibly loud rattle of an old Toyota Land Cruiser—and by its inhabitants. The woman in the back seat was veiled beneath a white shroud like every other white shroud in the town. But the driver—the driver was unmistakable. It was Mr. Bindar. And in that moment Claudia knew absolutely the identity of the woman in the back seat and her despair was replaced by the secret thrill of hope. She knew now, thanks to Sameera's gossip, that Mr. Bindar was not the criminal she had mistaken him to be. He and Martha were working together to save her; she knew this with the utmost certainty.

Claudia glanced at her companions, wondering if they had noticed the old Land Cruiser and the earless driver, hoping they had not seen what she had seen. But all three women were laughing at the sight of two goats copulating underneath the palms.

Never had Claudia been so happy to be ignored.

CHAPTER 8

The American ambassador to Turkey was having a minor fit. The Spode tureen that worked so well with his favorite china setting was chipped, unsuitable for guests who represented the most important museums of antiquities in the Western World. The sauce for his duck a l'orange would be disgraced served in anything else. Disgusted, the ambassador looked at the Turkish kitchen staff lined up in front of him and waited for a confession. Cleverly, each member of the staff simply looked confused. What other acts of sabotage might he discover from this group?

Losing what little patience he had left, the ambassador dismissed the staff and returned to the dining room to make sure the three flower arrangements that formed the table's centerpiece weren't drooping. One knew what to expect from Cyprus daffodils.

The daffodils were indeed drooping and one of the poppies was oozing pollen onto the lace tablecloth. Were poppies in bad taste? He snatched them out of the crystal bowl before they could do any more damage and wondered if it was too early to take more Advil.

Then the ambassador thought of the exquisite Byzantine cross he had acquired, the ivory worn to a breathtaking patina from centuries of adoration by the tired and soiled fingers of the faithful. How he got the antique would remain his secret, but that he possessed it now would be revealed to his envious guests that evening. He could hardly wait for his guests' restrained but covetous reactions.

One more problem to attend to and then he could put on his evening clothes. Would his new plaid cummerbund be too garish? Probably. But this was not so much an affair of state as it was a meeting of the cultured elite. And they were entitled to a bit of flair.

The annoying Captain Rappa was waiting in the front hall of the embassy. The ambassador's aide had been trying for days to get rid of him but his ridiculous persistence had overwhelmed the junior's ability to say "no." Now, on this busiest of afternoons, the ambassador himself would have to waste his precious time. Thank God no one would ever believe the captain's claim of a secret arrangement between the American and Algerian governments to return that pitiful girl to her royal father. And, thank God, it now appeared that the other witnesses, two American women and an annoying policeman of some sort, had been swallowed after her into the bowels of Algeria.

The ambassador angrily opened the double doors that protected the interior of the embassy from the front hall. He didn't have time for formalities or introductions or pleasantries.

"Captain Rappa," the ambassador said icily, "I understand there has been a misadventure on your ship because you made the serious mistake of choosing Algeria as a cruise destination. What did you think would find there? Certainly not hula girls with leis?"

The captain, it seemed, was not easily intimidated. "As you know," he announced, "the Swan II was commissioned by the United States to deliver…"

The ambassador raised his hand, an imperious demand for silence. "I have heard your silly story from Paul, my aide, so you needn't enumerate its implausible aspects again. We have filed a missing person's report through the Swedish embassy in Algeria and they will be on the lookout for wandering Americans. That's as much as we can do. I hope, Captain Rappa, that you use better judgment in the future."

The captain stepped forward; his face was suddenly quite red. "If our country can arrange the execution of a twenty year-old girl," he said, "it can arrange to have the two American citizens caught up in this tragedy returned to safety. I'm certain the *New York Times* foreign office, which I will visit shortly, will be very interested in the embassy's progress."

The annoying Captain Rappa finally had the ambassador's full attention. The ambassador decided to add a tone of parental concern to his reply. "Now," he said, "stop me if I am wrong, but I believe that the Swan II is in port in Izmir right now."

The captain nodded.

"Good. And do you know what a terrible time the Turkish Navy has been having trying to control the flow of heroin out of this country, especially out of that port? I'll tell you, Captain Rappa. The Turkish Navy has been having a very terrible time in spite of the fact that they've become more and more aggressive searching and disabling suspect ships."

The ambassador paused to gauge the effect his words were having on the old sailor. He noted the man's face had begun to lose its high color. Pleased, he went on.

"Since most of the heroin ends up in the United States, we try to help them out, giving them what little information we have, tips here and there about suspect traffickers. Of course, as you well know, the Turks don't recognize due process or habeas corpus, so they can act quickly, accelerating the sequence of discovery, arrest, and imprisonment. Sometimes the whole process takes place in a matter of hours."

Ah, yes, the ambassador thought, watching his guest's face freeze in shock and resisting the urge to grin. *The good captain has caught my full meaning.*

"Now," the ambassador went on, "don't you think it wise that you should leave Turkey before their navy, or for that matter, any other navy or even our own Coast Guard receives the wrong information about the Swan II? And believe me, Captain Rappa, if the Turks are determined to board, they will board."

The ambassador paused again, smiled politely, and then made what he thought was a most generous offer.

"Captain Rappa, know that I can arrange it so that nobody boards you in any water. I am offering you an opportunity, and it is one I strongly advise you not to refuse."

The captain made no reply.

"In the meantime," the ambassador went on, "I am sure the Swedish embassy will persuade Algeria to search diligently for your missing passengers. We will pray for their safety until their return."

With a practiced flair, the ambassador disappeared back through the double doors to the library, and slid them closed with a bang. He was largely confident that the whole nasty affair was over. The only thing that could go wrong now was the improbable rescue of the kidnapped American woman, and that ghastly little Nikkos had assured him as recently as yesterday that a rescue was impossible.

With a decisive nod of his head, the American ambassador to Turkey decided that the plaid cummerbund would be sensational.

CHAPTER 9

When the women returned to the palace it was late afternoon. Tahani insisted that she alone take Claudia back to her room. Once there, the door shut behind them, Tahani lifted the haik and fussed blindly underneath for Claudia's bound hands. When she had succeeded in untying them, she came around to face Claudia and reached up under the niqab for the knot of the gag. She untied that, too, and allowed Claudia to unveil herself. Finally, Tahani knelt and began to set Claudia's sore ankles free.

Tahani worked quickly as if, Claudia thought, trying to undo a mistake before being caught. Or, maybe, as if apologizing for the brutal treatment she had allowed earlier in the souk. When the shackles were gone, Tahani stood and tenderly brushed Claudia's cheek with the back of her hand. Claudia winced; she couldn't help it. And then Tahani took Claudia by the elbow and turned her toward the bed, toward the surprise that was lying behind the gauze curtains.

The cello.

Claudia looked at her captor and was almost moved by the look of excitement on the woman's face. Tahani seemed as excited to give Claudia this present as Claudia was to receive it. For a moment, in spite of the sores on the corners of her mouth, her numb fingers, the bruises on her ankles from hours in shackles, Claudia felt as if Tahani were a real friend. For a brief moment Claudia even wished that she could share the secret that was now curled safely away in her heart—that Martha had come for her. She wanted someone in this prison to care about her, just a little.

But Claudia said nothing. She knew that no one ever really would.

Tahani smiled and left Claudia alone.

CHAPTER 10

Mr. Bindar announced his presence in town by making an appointment with the mayor. There was no use expecting that he could drift into Djanet and not attract attention. An unidentified stranger would be alarming to Prince Jed al Hann and to Nikkos, if the pig were still around. The opposite course was best: Mr. Bindar would call as much attention to himself as possible. He would be an important businessman, an entrepreneur, someone that everyone, especially Prince Jed al Hann, needed to know. By an arrogant display of pretended connections to the industrialized interests of the Saudis, he hoped he would be drawn closer and closer to the American girl and to the blessing of judgement against the Mahdi.

As Dayak Oed, a representative of PanMediterania, a company with millions of Saudi dollars to invest, Mr. Bindar met with the mayor to discuss his company's use of a mining technology that would allow a heretofore unheard of method for the deep extraction of phosphates. He was sure that the mayor and, "May his name be praised," Prince Jed al Hann were concerned about the region's regrettably jejune mining activities and sure, too, that they might be interested in pursuing a fabulously profitable scheme, "Inshallah," to extract what riches were left in the Tassili Plateau. Finally, he informed the mayor that he could be reached at LaChambord, a hotel he trusted to provide comfort and privacy to the wife who was traveling with him.

Mr. Bindar had seen the mayor's type before. The man prided himself on being a dealmaker, the person in town to go to when a radiator for a 1983 Peugeot had rotted out or when a new refrigerator was needed. But the deal Mr. Dayak Oed had brought to him was much, much bigger. So the mayor put on his most indifferent air and declared that he was very busy but that perhaps he could find time to act as

PanMediterania's regional agent and arrange, as only he could, a meeting with Prince Jed al Hann.

As Mr. Bindar left the mayor's office he glanced back through the open door and saw the mayor nervously drilling a pencil deep inside his ear while, with the other hand, he dialed the phone.

Mr. Bindar and Martha had taken adjoining rooms at LaChambord the afternoon before the meeting with the mayor of Djanet. With its grand lobby and potted plants, its creaking wicker furniture and interior balconies, the hotel had about it a colonial, fin de siecle air. During some other lifetime, Martha would have found the hotel charming. But now, being any place except by Claudia's side was almost more than she could stand. She sensed Claudia nearby but felt horribly trapped by the hotel and by the convention of Muslim seclusion.

On the morning of Mr. Bindar's meeting, Martha anxiously picked at a breakfast of coffee, oranges, and rolls in her room before disappearing into the veil and exaggerated drapes of head-to-toe clothing. In spite of Mr. Bindar's cautions and her own reservations, Martha was determined to explore Djanet. Carefully, she descended the hotel's grand staircase. Once outside, Martha circled the outdoor market. At each individual stall she watched women identically veiled as she was bargain for flour, little sacks of spices, and bloody legs of mutton. A sudden downpour forced her to take refuge in the doorway of a mosque until she was yelled at by an old, shriveled man. Martha didn't understand his words but his intent was clear. A woman did not belong.

Martha walked on in the lessening rain and into the dimness of the souk. She stared deeply into the eyes of the veiled women she passed. Some stared back at her through the narrow slits in their white drapes; others quickly looked away. Twice Martha saw what she thought was a familiar stride, a just-right height and bearing. Twice she approached the veiled woman and whispered, "Claudia?", only to suffer the plunge from unreasonable hope to crushing disappointment.

Tired and thirsty, Martha walked on, lost in the souk's dizzying tunnels, alleys, and acute turns. Each step seemed to draw her further beyond any means of orientation or escape. Just as she had given up hope of ever finding her way out, of ever seeing the sky again, she emerged, the lone woman on the street, past curfew, and under the dangerous stares of a group of men smoking elaborate brass pipes while sitting on rickety chairs at tables they had dragged out of their adobe houses into the social dusk.

Hurriedly, Martha returned to the hotel to eat in silence with Mr. Bindar behind the curtained-off section of the dining room. She told him where she had been; she had to. He reprimanded her for leaving the hotel, for risking being discovered on the street past curfew. Martha listened to his admonishments and fought the impulse to cry, to cave into the despair of being so unapproachably close to Claudia and, at the same time, so impossibly far away.

The next day, their third in Djanet, Martha roamed the streets again. She reminded herself a hundred, a thousand times, of the futility of expecting an easy discovery, only to forget the lesson the moment she saw something familiar in the gait of the next veiled passerby. Once, while standing beneath the awning of a stall, Martha saw a pale, graceful hand emerge from within its haik cocoon to touch the bright brass of a bowl. It was as if in the dim tones of a canvas the painter had illuminated just these two objects, bowl and hand, so that they seemed to shine with their own internal light. Martha shouldered her way past the other shrouded women at the stall so that she could touch the beautiful hand, but when she did it jerked away, disappearing inside its formless drapes.

At the end of the day, before curfew, Martha returned to the hotel, hungry and exhausted. Mr. Bindar frowned but said no more about her risky behavior. Martha sat across from him at their table and poked at her dinner. She knew with utter certainty that her efforts to find

Claudia simply by wandering the streets were futile. And at the same time she knew, with as much certainty, that unless Claudia was found, she would wander the streets of Djanet forever.

CHAPTER 11

Claudia woke the next morning feeling that the world was beginning to reassemble itself. Martha was in Djanet. She had come for her, and until then, Claudia would wait with as much patience as she could muster and play the cello. It had the presence in the bedroom of a family member, a loved one who had come to be with her in the hospital before surgery. It was a relief from gnawing homesickness.

The night before, after returning from the excursion to the souk, Claudia's fingers had been too numb to play. So she had shined the lovely instrument with the haik she had found on the bed, and then tuned it, rubbed resin on the bowstrings, and inhaled the particular scent of the wood. It was the smell of home, of Martha, of the Maine farm, and Claudia had wept with longing.

But that next morning, Claudia could tell that her fingers were limber again, and for the first time in her weeks of captivity, she was able to greet the new day with some eagerness.

Still in her nightgown, she slid the little bench away from the dressing table. It was a bit too low but it would have to do. Then she brought the cello to the bench and opened her legs to it so that it pushed the silk of her nightgown almost all the way up her thighs. The cello's slim neck brushed past her lace-covered breast and settled into her shoulder. And then Claudia began to play. Brahms. It was the perfect expression of the sadness of the captive, her forlorn longing for Martha, and her abiding trust that everything would some day be all right.

Outside the birds in the aviary rose and fussed and settled onto new perches, lizards sunned themselves on mud walls, and beyond, Imam called the faithful to prayer. And the wisps of Brahms evaporated into the morning sky.

CHAPTER 12

Mr. Bindar had studied both palaces, driving past them as slowly as he dared. He tried to see over the high walls or through the elaborate gates, to make out what he could of the buildings he knew were hidden in the lush crowns of palms. He surveyed the perimeters, searching for the best means of penetration and escape.

The first problem was to find out which palace housed Miss Simmerhorn. He had learned in town that Prince Jed al Hann had divided his family between the two households. In one, a Mediterranean-style mansion built right along the road in town behind an eight-foot fence, he kept his mother and two wives, both of whom had given him daughters. In the other, the one that looked like a garish, well-fortified Moorish castle overlooking the town, he kept his youngest wife and his two remaining daughters. Mr. Bindar desperately hoped that Miss Simmerhorn was not being kept in this seemingly impenetrable fortress.

Once the first problem could be solved, Mr. Bindar would have to deal with the second. He would have to find out where exactly within the particular palace Miss Simmerhorn was confined. Both residences were far too big for Mr. Bindar to conduct a one-man, run-amok search. By the time he got close to Miss Simmerhorn, hundreds of guards would have been alerted. Before going in he needed to have narrowed the search to a wing, a floor, a tower. That information would make his chances, as his father would have said, "Friendlier to Allah."

But neither problem had been solved yet. The mayor undoubtedly held all of the information that Mr. Bindar needed to know; the man was an expert at harvesting every grain of information that came his way and later selling or exchanging it for profit in the form of money or favors. Mr. Bindar knew that at the right time he would learn what he needed to know from the mayor. He also knew that his asking right out for such information would be deadly.

Mr. Bindar had counseled patience for Martha. Now, he found his own counsel difficult to follow. He would at least wait to meet the prince. The man might unwittingly reveal something Mr. Bindar could use. And if not?

Mr. Bindar sighed. He was all too sure that eventually there would be more violence.

CHAPTER 13

Zora had a fist-sized ball of hashish and an obligation to make sure that Nikkos could get into Claudia's room. Tonight wouldn't work. Sameera had already asked for her help with the American filth. But the next afternoon would be perfect.

Zora's hands shook as she shaved a bit of the gummy resin into the bowl of her little pipe. *Sameera tonight*, she thought, *the Mahdi tomorrow. Maybe I, too, will have fun with the American while she is in our power.*

CHAPTER 14

Mr. Bindar was informed that the meeting with Prince Jed al Hann was set for noon the next day. The mayor himself would drive the prince for a lunch at the hotel.

"Mssr. Oed," the mayor said, fairly oozing self-satisfaction, "I do what no one else can do. The prince comes himself because I ask him to. You and I have agreement, oui? We are partners? Without me, you go home with empty hands, never meet the right people. Now, inshallah, the mines will be rich again, you are rich because of me so I am rich, too. Oui?"

Mr. Bindar observed the mayor of Djanet. His face was red and perspiring; his casual familiarity seemed an uncomfortable combination of a plea and a threat. Mr. Bindar nodded and wondered how many other arrangements the man had contrived that had come to the same end this one would. Begrudgingly, he admired the mayor's ability to sustain hope, day after day, scheme after scheme, in this town of goats and mud and feudal palaces.

"Of course," Mr. Bindar said, with the smooth assurance of the powerfully connected Mssr. Oed. "Of course you are entitled to a share of the wealth. You may count on it."

CHAPTER 15

Claudia played, undisturbed, most of the morning. Curiously, Sameera had not come in as she usually did, carrying the ribbons which gaily fluttered like streamers but which were as tight as cords when tied around Claudia's wrists. The collar was on its peg, and even the servant who brought her breakfast hadn't bothered to lock the door after leaving the tray behind.

For the first time Claudia was free to leave her room, even go into the gardens. But she didn't. She played. Dvorak and Bach and Purcell, Berlin and Corelli and Handel. She need not have the collar off or the door unlocked to feel exuberant. Martha had come. And until then, when they were reunited, in her music and heart Claudia was free, truly free.

In the late afternoon the servant brought in a little tray of food. She came back an hour later, as she did every day, with a folded pile of clean bath towels, always pink, always smelling of cinnamon. The servant had never looked at Claudia; there had not been one moment of eye contact since the day she had arrived at the palace. Claudia had tried smiling, nodding, even stepping in her way so the woman would at least have to acknowledge her presence, but the servant was too numbed by caste or dictate to respond. Even now, with Vivaldi singing in the air, the servant did not look away from her tasks.

But the routine was different this afternoon. After the towels had been put away in the huge, tiled bathroom, the woman began to run a bath for Claudia in the deep, spa-sized marble tub. When she had adjusted the golden knobs for the right temperature, she left, this time locking the door behind her.

Was Claudia being told to take a bath? Was there an event for which she was to prepare? Her mild curiosity plunged into terror when

the door opened again. Sameera and Zora stood in the doorway holding leather cuffs and straps.

And with terrified revulsion, Claudia recognized a bridle, just like
the one that had gagged the poor, captive girl on the ship.

CHAPTER 16

Claudia sat on the soaking ledge around the bottom of the tub, up to her neck in the warm and sudsy water. Zora had buckled the bit into her mouth and held its straps over the side of the tub. When Claudia moved the wrong way or twisted, Sameera yelled and Zora yanked Claudia back into submission.

Sameera, too, was in the tub with Claudia. She cooed as she rubbed bubbles over Claudia's breasts, down and around her thighs and buttocks, between her legs. That is until a look of deep hatred on Claudia's face annoyed her so much she commanded Zora to drop a heavy towel over Claudia's head.

Sameera wasn't satisfied for long. She wanted to wash Claudia's cheeks with the fat sponge and then the sides of her delicate nose, behind her lovely ears, the length of her graceful neck. Sameera grabbed the towel and petulantly threw it to the floor. Claudia winced as Sameera screamed an order loud enough to be heard through the bedroom and out into the hall. In a moment the servant was standing next to the tub with a scarf in her hands. Zora pulled Claudia's head back with the straps of the bridle so the servant could easily blindfold her.

And Sameera was happy. Once again she could wash and play with her exquisite captive.

When the bath was over, Zora pulled Claudia to her feet. Still holding the straps, Zora made her hold still, and then turn around, and then stand with her legs farther apart so Sameera could dry there, too, far up between.

Next they led Claudia, naked and still wearing the blindfold, into the bedroom. She sensed one of the women part the gauze curtains around the bed. Then Zora, unmistakably Zora, turned her around and pushed her onto the edge of the bed. Only then did Zora drop the reins; a moment later Claudia heard her leave the room. Claudia could tell that Sameera stood directly in front of her.

Nothing happened for a moment. Claudia tried for control, took deep, calming breaths. She wasn't even willing to jeopardize the fragment of peace by reaching up for her blindfold. But the moment shattered, as she knew it would.

Zora returned. Suddenly, she was behind Claudia, wrenching her arms across the bed and up toward the massive bedposts. Claudia tried to pull away, but now Sameera was pulling on her wrists. Claudia imagined Sameera reaching for a rope while Zora held her arm. She felt the rope chafe the delicate skin of her wrist as Sameera tied it around and around. Claudia knew what was next. Sameera tied first one wrist and then the other to each of the two top bedposts. When she was done, Claudia's arms were stretched out as far as the tendons allowed.

Claudia kicked out, but the rest of the procedure was easy and soon her legs were bound the same way to the posts at the foot of the bed. Spread-eagled, Claudia arched and screamed past the bit still buckled in her mouth, but her resistance was now pathetic and painful.

Claudia lay still, her chest heaving. She imagined Zora and Sameera, her despicable torturers, standing back and marveling at their captive's complete, stretched-out vulnerability. Then she could tell by the smell of hashish that Zora was over her again. She laughed and grabbed Claudia by the ends of the bit, jerking her head up off the bed. When she shoved Claudia's head back down there was a pillow underneath. And then Claudia heard both women leave the room.

Moments passed. Claudia wondered if she could will herself to sleep or better still, to unconsciousness. But before she could even try to mentally escape the torture chamber, Sameera was back.

The girl climbed on the bed and straddled her. The smell of her heavy, cloying perfume made Claudia feel sick.

"Lift your head," Sameera whispered. "I take off gag and blindfold now. Your poor mouth looks so sore. I put cream on it. We are lovers now. You be good."

Claudia was all too eager for the bridle to be removed; the pain it caused was brutal. More, she wanted Sameera to see both the disgust and the terror she felt, mirrored in her eyes. And though she knew it would accomplish nothing, she wanted to scream and yell and beg for mercy.

She lifted her head as high as she could so that Sameera could easily reach the buckle and the knot. And when the girl had released her, Claudia let her head fall back down on the pillow, ready for this chance to look directly up into Sameera's face, to confront her captor, to say something, anything at all. But all she could do was look away and sob.

Sameera was prepared for the boudoir. Her hair was combed and shining. She had applied heavy but artful make-up to her girlish face. And instead of her usual garb, she wore a short, white silk nightie straight from Victoria's Secret; the lace at the bosom was embroidered with pearls. Cut flowers had been arranged in the room sometime while Claudia was being bathed. Bowls of incense smoked on every surface; candles, hundreds of them, illuminated the otherwise dark room. The women had created a veritable Vegas honeymoon suite.

Claudia commanded herself to stop crying and resisted the urge to scream for help or to yell in frustration. The whole thing was absurd. This room, this child. Claudia's brain simply refused to believe that now, alone with Sameera, she couldn't overpower her abuser with reason.

"Sameera," she began. Her throat was raw and the skin at the corners of her mouth felt split. "Sameera, please, please let's just stop now. Untie me, Sameera. Let me up. It's wrong to force someone to do what she doesn't want to do. Do you understand? It's wrong to tie me up and to hurt me this way. I would never do this to you. Untie me and we'll still spend the evening together. We'll talk, like friends. Just untie me. If you don't we will never be friends again and for the rest of your life you'll think about this night and you'll feel ashamed. Please."

Sameera's expression was bland. Claudia dared to hope she had gotten through to the child. And then Sameera slapped her hand over Claudia's mouth and squeezed firmly. "If you talk anymore," she said,

"I will gag you again. You are too pretty to wear a gag so don't make me." She squeezed harder. "Do you promise to be quiet? Just nod if you do." Sameera, the pupper-master, moved Claudia's head up and down with the pressure of her hand.

Claudia looked up at the girl, over her ringed fingers. Once again her eyes filled with tears.

Sameera released Claudia and slipped the nightie over her head. At the sight of the naked girl Claudia turned away but Sameera grabbed her chin and yanked her head back into place on the pillow. Then, she balled the nightie and shoved it into Claudia's mouth.

Sameera lay down, her head nestled between Claudia's breasts, and with her fingertips made light spirals in Claudia's scented pubic hair.

Loving foreplay.

CHAPTER 17

As she had for the four previous mornings, Martha wandered the souk, looking through the narrow slits in her heavy, formless drapes into dark, unfamiliar eyes that stared back, curious or contemptuous, or that looked away, embarrassed by her aggressive, silent inquiry. Each encounter was a little explosion of hope, followed by a little explosion of despair.

Finally, Martha came out from the dim, twisting streets of the souk and into the market square. It began to rain and she took refuge under the awning of a deserted stall. Each palm surrounding the square became a muffled percussion instrument, its fronds like shiny drumheads being beaten by the raindrops. The rain grew heavier and the tempo increased, gradually becoming a low roar, like an endless freight train passing somewhere just out of sight. Directly across from her in a pen made of sticks, a dozen sheep shifted and bawled; Martha could smell their wet wool even through her niqab. And then the Imam began, calling the faithful to prayer, their voices amplified by the tinny speakers on their minarets. Martha felt that the morning itself was forlorn, deserted.

And then a slight, humid breeze brought—a sound. It was faint, far away, not quite tangible. It was vague, uneasy, a phantom. The sound was gone and then it was there, and then gone again.

Recklessly ignoring decorum, Martha pulled off her head covering, untied her niqab, and listened hard. It was there again. The sound. Yes, unmistakable. A cello. It could only be coming from the palace up on the hill.

And then Martha knew. Claudia was there.

CHAPTER 18

Martha hurried back to find Mr. Bindar. Claudia was excruciatingly close; there was no time to waste.

Mr. Bindar was not in his room at LaChambord. Martha decided to wait for him in her own room next door. Each creak of the hotel's stairs, each door banging closed in the hotel's depths, was a cause for hope and then, when Mr. Bindar still did not come, an unbearable disappointment. Martha waited, her head and face uncovered but still in her haik, hoping to be going out again soon, very soon, to rescue her love.

After an endless hour Martha heard the door to her room open. She was so excited that Mr. Bindar had finally arrived she didn't even stop to wonder why he hadn't knocked, as was his habit. She turned toward the door to meet him, to thank him for what he had already done and for what together they could now finish.

And then, all color, all sound, all sensation were instantaneously drained out of the world, replaced by one thing: Nikkos' hyena leer.

"Oh, Miss Bekele," he said mockingly, "may I get you something, turn down your bed, bring you more ice? Perhaps I can bring you Miss Simmerhorn's ear? Or maybe her tit?" Slowly, with deliberation, the little man produced a long, curved knife from his belt, closed the door behind him, and moved into the room.

Martha was paralyzed. For a moment all she wanted was for Nikkos to finish whatever ghastly deed he had come to perform.

"The mayor," he went on in an oily way, "he tells me about man from mining company and his wife. 'We all make money,' he says. I think 'maybe yes, maybe no.' I too smart so I come to see for myself."

Nikkos picked up Martha's discarded niqab from the bed and smelled it. "Tomorrow," he said, "I fuck your friend like the pig she is, and while I have her down I will tell her that I have cut your throat. I will show her your blood on this." Nikkos shook the veil at Martha and took another step closer.

Somehow, Martha found the ability to take a few steps backwards, into the corner of the room. She wanted to wretch or to scream, but she was rendered mute by terror.

He was ten feet away now. She could smell him, see the stains on his shirt and down the front of his pants.

"You will bleed to death," Nikkos said, grinning madly. "I know how to do this slowly. Watch the knife, Miss Bekele. You are not too good for Nikkos now are you?"

He was less than three steps from Martha. He raised the knife and reached for her with his other hand when suddenly, an explosion opened a hole in the front of Martha's haik.

The first shot hit a table lamp, but the next hit him in the throat. For a frozen moment Martha saw Nikkos' mouth drop open in pain and in shock, and in his eyes there was a plea for help. For a frozen moment Nikkos looked once again like the servile little steward from the Swan II. But the moment melted and Nikkos was again a murderer, slashing at Martha with the instinct of a sadist.

Another bullet hit him in the mouth. The next, over the left eye socket, dropped him and he curled on the floor, his hands over his face, whimpering.

But it couldn't end there. Too much had been wrong for too long. Martha took the silver.380 automatic out from underneath her haik, pointed it at Nikkos' chest, and fired the gun's final two shots. Only then was the nightmare finally over.

Martha stumbled past the mangled body to the other side of the room and began to sob. Her tears came in choking, convulsive waves; the dam that had been holding them back since Claudia's abduction had finally burst.

When the door opened Martha's head jerked up. The only thing she saw through her tears was an Uzi. And then Mr. Bindar's arms were around her and she was crying into his shoulder.

After a few minutes her sobs slowed but she continued to cling to Mr. Bindar.

"What you have done is very bad," he said to her gently. "Very bad. I was supposed to do that. I have been waiting very patiently for my opportunity to kill him."

Martha smiled into his shoulder, then pulled back to look into his face.

"Guess what else I've done?" she said. "I've found Claudia."

CHAPTER 19

The desk clerk decided to put his shoes back on. He had taken them off almost an hour earlier to say his prayers, but now his feet were getting cold. He had just finished slipping on the second shoe when he heard the shots.

"More of the trouble," he thought, but he had survived the French, the Armed Islamic Group, the army, the Islamic Salvation Front, the FLN, Libyans, even Christian missionaries by minding his own business, and he wasn't about to change now.

He hit the desk bell hard, twice, as if hoping it would drown out the noise from above, and waited for the annoying Hausa cripple who worked ineffectively as bellhop and kitchen help to come. When he finally arrived, the desk clerk snarled at him.

"Bring my newspaper and hot tea. And remember, you heard no noise a few minutes ago in room twenty-six. Understand?"

Only Allah knew what kind of a mess they would find up there in the morning.

CHAPTER 20

"I'll train you to be more grateful, to pleasure me the way I try to pleasure you," Sameera complained with a pout. She leaned over Claudia, still tied to the bed, and shoved the nightie back into Claudia's mouth, deep. And then, she was gone.

Time passed. Claudia was able to turn her head enough to see out the windows into the aviary and beyond, into the now dark sky. She tried to stay relaxed, to let her arms and legs stretch out naturally so that the ropes wouldn't pull, but she ached and the aches turned into cramps. She worked on thrusting out the nightie with her tongue so she that could call for Tahani, for anybody. Just as the last piece of wet silk was out, the servant entered the room.

Claudia lifted her head off the deep pillow and whispered "Please" in a language that needed no interpretation.

The servant ignored her plea. She took the collar off its little peg and motioned for Claudia to lift her head so that she could fasten it. When this was done, she uncoiled the chain, attached one end to the collar and the other around the foot of the bed. Finally, she began to untie Claudia, her legs first and then her arms. The entire ugly process was conducted matter-of-factly, as if it were a mundane housecleaning chore.

The servant locked the door behind her when she left. Slowly, stiffly, Claudia got out of the bed and looked for something to put on. She found only a giant bath towel and wrapped it around her, knotting it above her sore breasts.

Claudia waited for some emotion to overwhelm her, but stronger than any feeling of repugnancy or rage was the bleak feeling of being alone in place where no one cared, where no one would ever care.

Martha might be close, but until Claudia was reunited with her, nothing could protect her. Maybe nothing could protect her ever again.

But there was her cello. Claudia walked to the little bench, chain rattling after her. She could have removed the collar around her neck. It wasn't locked, but it didn't seem to matter anymore. All that mattered was her beloved cello. She sat on the bench and stiffly cradled it. And then she began to play a little Mozart piece, oblivious to the tears streaming down her face.

CHAPTER 21

Martha and Mr. Bindar stopped at the mayor's home. While Martha waited in the back seat of the car, Mr. Bindar went inside and told the mayor that the prince, so anxious to begin negotiations with PanMediterania, had requested their presence that very night. They must leave immediately.

The mayor swelled with importance and requested a moment to prepare. Mr. Bindar agreed and returned to the Toyota. The mayor finally emerged. When he was still yards from the car Martha smelled his rancid aftershave. The mayor placed his hand on the handle of the car—and then he spotted Martha. She watched him puff up with indignation, his sense of propriety offended by the presence of this veiled woman who would accompany them on this important mission.

"You should not bring her," the mayor said brusquely. "She has no business with us. We are going to the palace of Prince Jed al Hann and you will offend him. Things are different down here. She can wait here with the women of my household."

"No," Mr. Bindar replied firmly. "I want to take her. She has been in her room all day and needs to go for a ride. She's like my pet goat, takes up room but at least she has good milk."

Martha rolled her eyes and felt an almost irresistible urge to giggle, but sobered immediately when she thought of the blood and the shattered bone left behind in the hotel.

"No, I do not ride with a woman to Prince Jed al Hann's," the mayor said angrily. "She must get out."

"And you must get in, now," Mr. Bindar replied coldly. Suddenly, an Uzi was aimed directly into the mayor's crotch. "Or there will be two women in this car."

Martha could no longer see the mayor's face, but when he slumped into the front seat of the car, he seemed much smaller than he had sounded. His aftershave threatened to choke her.

Mr.Bindar explained what the mayor was to do: give him an introduction to get them past the guards and into the palace, the one on the hill. Did the mayor know if the prince was there? "No." Did he know where in the palace the American girl was being kept?

"How did you know she was there?" the mayor demanded. Mr. Bindar did not answer so the mayor nervously continued. "She is in the oda with the other women, where they belong." He looked disdainfully over his shoulder at Martha, and then back to Mr. Bindar. "You're not from PanMediterania, are you?"

Under the circumstances it was question that seemed truly pathetic, and really, not a question at all but an awful realization. Martha almost felt sorry for the self-important mayor. Almost.

Silently, Mr. Bindar drove up the hill towards the palace. From the back seat, Martha now held the Uzi firmly against the back of the mayor's neck. When they got close to the top of the hill, Mr. Bindar stopped the Toyota, retrieved the Uzi from Martha, and the three walked the rest of the way up a sandy path to the palace grounds. The gates were open and as soon as they had passed through, the front of the palace was flooded with security lights.

Martha stared. The palace was huge and almost perfectly round. To Martha it had all the dubious charm of a squat stone tower. Instead of windows there were medieval archers' slots, and three stories up, the top of the structure had been finished with faux battlements. Martha saw two guards patrolling the grounds at some distance. They were dressed in fatigues and black berets, their outfits comically inappropriate for this architecture reminiscent of the Middle Ages. The guards looked nothing like noble Moors or knights errant; they simply looked like thugs with machineguns.

Martha, the mayor, and Mr. Bindar crossed the grounds to the palace. Martha watched as the mayor shot a look at the two patrol guards and then a look at Mr. Bindar, as if choosing between the threat of the guards' Klasnikovs or Mr. Bindar' s Uzi. The Uzi won.

Mr. Bindar pounded on the huge doors made out of rough wood and decorated with hundreds of iron studs. After a moment the doors swung open and two guards dressed in royal blue uniforms stared belligerently out at them. Martha's courage almost failed her.

The mayor immediately offered the guards a frenzied explanation Arabic, and while Martha could not understand a single word, the essence of the obsequious man's speech was clear.

"The Prince Jed al Hann, my friend, Insalada, and now my partner in an undertaking that would restore wealth and power to all the faithful, had requested that he—who had been here many times as a guest and was known, as the Prince was, but to a lesser degree of course since the Prince was unmatched in his kindness, for his generosity, too, and had, in fact brought many gifts in the past for the Prince to use and share with those as devoted as he himself was . . ."

Martha was frightened but she couldn't help smiling underneath her veil at the mayor's servile, breathless monologue. She glanced over at Mr. Bindar and saw that he, too, was grimly amused by the mayor's barely coherent babble.

The mayor went on. "For instance, the Ramadan fireworks just last year—the Prince requested that he bring the president of PanMediterania here, this night because Allah, his name forever be praised, himself would wish it so, although why his wife came with him was as strange to him as it must be to you who serve the Prince so well and in any case was just another example of how far people in the North had plunged into the void of the unfaithful the way the rest of the world had but not here, May Allah be praised, because of the Prince and the faithful who served him as he did and that was why on this night he was willing to come and even walk part way out of reverence for the sanctity of the Prince's magnificent palace and his peace, Insalada, a peace that only the most devout and beneficent and strong and wise and prescient could know, a wonder unto itself and cause to give birth every moment to hope and the blessings of Allah, may his name be praised."

While the mayor was prattling his soliloquy of devotion, Martha looked up at the tower. Silhouetted in one of the dim, narrow slots three stories directly above them was a woman's face. It looked down at them for just a moment and was gone. Somehow Martha knew that the face did not belong to Claudia, but to someone who was keeping Claudia captive against her will. Martha could hardly endure being so close to the moment when Claudia, somewhere within the walls of the dread palace, would see her again and would know just how much Martha loved her.

If I am to die tonight, she prayed, to whoever or whatever would listen, *please let me see Claudia one more time before the end.*

Martha could see the disgust on the guards' faces at the mayor's fawning. They were resisting, just barely Martha thought, the impulse to bully him, probably because they knew that indeed the mayor had done numerous, petty favors for the prince. But Martha could also tell that they were confused by the mayor's request. They looked to one another and shook their heads and shrugged.

For the first time Martha noticed that Mr. Bindar looked more anxious than confident. He leaned over to her and softly interpreted what the guards were saying.

"The prince is not here," he said. "He is at his other residence and is not expected back all week. Why would he tell these people to meet him here? And the ugly man and his wife make them nervous. Maybe she is part of the negotiations, another gift from the mayor, and the prince doesn't want her seen anywhere but here? She has pretty eyes. Scared, eyes. The prince would like that."

The guards now told the mayor that he and the ugly man and the dark woman could wait just inside while a call was made to the prince. Maybe he would be here soon. Maybe not. In either case they would be locked in.

The guards pushed hard to open the massive doors all the way. Martha reluctantly crossed the threshold into the entrance hall. And when the guards had closed and locked the doors behind them, she felt as if she had descended into one of the lower circles of hell.

They stood in a grand, stone room, the ceiling about twenty feet high. Almost every square inch of wall was adorned with antlers and horns. One entire wall was occupied by a rack of six-foot elephant tusks, each capped at the tip and base in gold or silver. They were displayed as crossed pairs, giant ivory x'es. On another wall were rhinoceros heads, beginning at eye level and jammed all the way to the ceiling, their horns thrusting out into the room, making the wall look like a long-thorned hedge. The third wall was a chaos of carnage: kudu, impala, Oryx, ibex, gnu, buffalo, rabbit-sized dik-dik, antelope, duiker, eland, even elk and moose. If it had once grown an antler or horn, it had been killed for its antler and horn.

On the far wall next to double doors identical to the ones through which they had entered were claws and fangs and boar tusks, each set mounted in a mahogany frame, the frames jammed against each other from floor to ceiling.

The room contained no furniture, no rugs or pillows or cushions. Nothing relieved the grotesque welcome to the palace of Prince Jed al Hann. Even Mr. Bindar was clearly shocked by the spectacle and looked at Martha with incredulous revulsion.

But just for a moment. Then his Uzi was out and he was pulling on the handles of the interior doors. Martha was not surprised to learn that they were locked but she was not willing to admit defeat, either, not when she was so close to Claudia.

"Here," she said, "I'll try." She tugged on the iron handles, hoping for some magic touch, hoping for an escape from the macabre animal mausoleum.

The doors didn't budge. Martha turned and saw the mayor smirking at her. She looked desperately to Mr. Bindar for help.

"Miss Bekele," he said gravely, "soon the guards will find out that we are intruders, that the prince really hasn't sent for us." He gave another, futile tug at the interior doors. "I can't shoot them open," he said. "And now, there is nothing else left to do but to wait."

The mayor laughed. Martha doubted he understood English but she was sure he understood the bleakness of the situation.

Martha thought about Claudia, so close and yet still so far. She hoped that Claudia knew just how much she loved her. She hoped that someday, somehow Claudia would know just how close she had come to rescuing her. Though maybe to know that would only hurt Claudia.

Suddenly, Martha was tired of the whole charade. She began to remove her head covering and niqab but Mr. Bindar took her hand, his shoulders bowed with the shame of failure.

"Miss Bekele," he said softly, "stay dressed, stay covered. You are untouchable that way. When they come for us they will come from the outside. I will shoot as many as I can and they will try to shoot me. When this is happening, just lie on the floor. You won't get killed. So stay there. Don't try to run. You have no place to go. Maybe you will get to see your friend and maybe they will send you home some day. Maybe I can shoot enough that we can get away, but don't try to run without me. I know where to go. I have people waiting. It would be impossible for you by yourself."

Mr. Bindar's eyes were shiny with tears and Martha's heart broke yet again.

"We have tried," he said. "You have been very brave, and we have come so close. Your friend is very lucky for your devotion. Please forgive me for failing."

Martha pulled Mr. Bindar to her and rested her head on his shoulder. "There was no trying without you, Mr. Bindar. You gave me the most precious gift in the world. Hope. I will always love you for that." Slowly, Martha pulled away.

Several long minutes later Martha heard footsteps and a lock turn. The footsteps had come from inside the palace, and it was the inside lock that had been turned.

The Mayor screamed, then shrieked his name and no doubt called for help. Mr. Bindar grabbed Martha and pushed her to the floor, out of direct sight of the door. Then he lay on the stone floor directly to the left of the door, the Uzi aimed.

The door opened slowly, just enough to clear the latch; then, cautiously, it opened all the way. Martha held her breath. Mr. Bindar leapt to his feet, the Uzi pointed at the intruder.

There stood a woman, alone. She wore a long, black jersey smock, like a graduation robe. That, with her black hair and heavy eyebrows and dark eyes made her look like a shadow.

"You must come with me quickly," she whispered. "I have sent everyone away looking for a golden camel, but they will be back soon."

Martha didn't understand a word of the Arabic, but from somewhere beyond, perhaps on the other side of the tiled courtyard around which the palace was built, perhaps one or two stories above the carnage room, Martha did hear and understand—Mozart.

Mr. Bindar's face became animated with delight and he lowered the Uzi, almost in apology, and gestured for Martha to rise.

The mayor looked dumfounded. He stepped forward to follow the woman, but Mr. Bindar shoved him back into the macabre horn room and locked the heavy doors on the mayor's hysterical cries.

Mr. Bindar and Martha followed the woman to a courtyard, and for a moment they were underneath the dome of a starry sky. They continued past plants growing around a pool, a miniature jungle, and then up a flight of exposed stone stairs on the other side of the courtyard. At the top there was another locked door, and from behind it, the sounds of Mozart, louder than before. Martha desperately wanted to call to Claudia. Mr. Bindar, sensing her excitement, touched her arm and put his finger to his lips.

The woman, their guide, opened the door with a key and beckoned them forward. Martha couldn't think clearly; her breath came faster and faster. They passed through a lounge, all carpets and divans and the pungent smell of incense. A fountain bubbled in the middle of the room. Next to it, a coarse woman slept noisily, as if drunk, on a pile of cushions.

Martha and Mr. Bindar followed their guide across to yet another locked door. The Mozart was louder and still, just on the other side. Suddenly, before their guide could fit a key into the lock, another woman, quite young, ran into the room shrieking in desperate ululations. Before Martha could react, Mr. Bindar turned, grabbed the young woman, and hit her just once in the stomach. Immediately, she dropped onto a pile of rugs, gasping for breath.

Gasps. The bubbling of the fountain. Mozart.

And then their guide unlocked the final door.

CHAPTER 22

Not very often in life is the burden of accumulated sorrow punctured by a shining moment of absolute, exquisite relief. And when it is, there is no script to follow, no conditioned response.

So it was for Martha when Tahani unlocked and opened the final door and she saw Claudia there before her. Sorrow was pierced by joy so exquisite it was beyond expression. Martha was frozen in the doorway. She stared at Claudia, wanting to go to her but absolutely unable to transcend through action the euphoria of reunion.

Claudia, my beautiful Claudia, she thought, *what have they done to you?*

Claudia was sitting on the edge of a large bed wearing just a towel and a horrible leather collar. She looked so little, so broken.

Claudia raised her head. And Martha knew that Claudia saw only another captor, another woman draped in formless hijab, staring at her.

And then, Claudia's eyes brightened. She got up from the bed with somnambulistic slowness, placed the cello gently on the floor, and waited, her hands held out, palms up, at waist level.

Martha dashed forward and gently took Claudia's hands. She stood at arms length so that they could look into each other's eyes. Then Martha tenderly unbuckled the collar from around her loved one's neck. Then Claudia tenderly unveiled her loved one's face. And then they were tight in each other's arms.

Their guide looked at the floor and spoke. Mr. Bindar translated for Martha and Claudia.

"My name is Tahani. The American, she was treated very badly here and it shames me. But you must get out right now. When I leave I will lock the door while you go out this way."

Mr. Bindar followed Tahani over to a deep, empty closet. She pressed against the closet's back panel and it slid open onto a narrow, steep stairwell. Tahani turned back to Mr. Bindar.

"The Prince," she said, faint sarcasm in her voice, "used to bring his Mali whores in this way so we wouldn't see them. It leads down to the aviary and there you will find a screen door to the outside."

Tahani came back into the room and took Claudia gently out of Martha's arms. "You must not go outside like that," she said, as Mr. Bindar continued to translate. "An undressed woman in Djanet would not get far. You must wear my abayya."

"You will certainly be going with us," Mr. Bindar said then, and Martha nodded in agreement. "You can't stay here now."

Tahani's reply came readily. "She says," Mr. Bindar explained, "that she will be fine here. She is carrying the prince's son and so is very special to him. He would never harm her. And besides, he would not have liked what was happening to the American. She says she knows that the prince is your enemy but he is in the eyes of Allah always. And he shines there. Still, she urges us to make haste."

Mr. Bindar turned away while Tahini removed her abayya and handed it to Claudia. Claudia touched Tahani lightly on the shoulder, in thanks, before turning away.

CHAPTER 23

A ground hornbill saw that the aviary door had been left opened and, picking up a twig in its ridiculously elaborate bill, walked out of its cage. Ahead of the hornbill, Mr. Bindar, Martha, and Claudia had disappeared into the night.

"We can't get back to the car," Mr. Bindar said firmly, as soon as they were outside the palace grounds. "All the guards will go to the front the palace, and that will be the very bad place to be. But my days of reconnaissance might pay off."

Mr. Bindar led the women to a dry wash behind the palace. One by one they scrambled down a bank of loose stones, slipping and stumbling on the skree. When all three had reached the bottom, Martha caught Claudia's hand, insisting for a moment on her full attention.

"Tell me how you feel, Claudia," she whispered. "Can you do this?"

Claudia kissed her quickly on the forehead. "I have never," she said, "felt so perfectly awful and so perfectly wonderful in all my life."

And in spite of the sores around the corners of Claudia's mouth and the harsh lines etched around Claudia's eyes, Martha thought her loved one's face had never looked more beautiful.

The bottom of the wash was strewn with boulders. "This is our route into town," Mr. Bindar explained. "It meanders all over the place but it will get us there, I promise. But now we must keep going."

Suddenly, the palace behind them burst into floodlit illumination and the sky was aglow. The harsh sounds of shouting and engines starting and sirens wailing pierced their ears.

The prisoners had been discovered missing.

"Come!" Mr. Bindar commanded.

For the next forty minutes or so the three worked their way over sharp rocks, tripping in the dark, bruising their feet, twisting their ankles. But they kept on, knowing that each painful step brought them closer and closer to safety. They hoped.

Suddenly, Mr. Bindar halted. "I fall behind," he explained hoarsely. "You two go on. If anybody gets close, I can slow them down. If you hear me shoot, hide as best you can until I catch up with you. And if . . ."

He didn't finish his sentence. He didn't have to. Martha knew just how dire a situation they were in. If Mr. Bindar was killed, Martha and Claudia most likely would be captured. And then . . .

The women went on. At certain points the wash became terribly shallow, and they crouched as they went so that their heads could not be seen from above. At other points the wash became terribly deep and they felt as if they were running through a canyon whose walls reached to the heavens.

After a time Martha ceased to hear any noise from behind them, from the direction of the palace. She dared to feel a moment of relief, to believe that she and Claudia might yet escape the prince's men. And then, as if to mock her, from just ahead came a cacophony of vicious snarls and yelps. Claudia grasped Martha's arm and the two women froze.

"It is all right."

Martha whirled around to see Mr. Bindar hulking in the gloom.

"I am sorry to scare you," he whispered. He pushed past Martha and Claudia and motioned for them to follow him. He led them about another one hundred feet down the wash and stopped at the ridge of a crater that Martha thought might have been formed by a bomb. In the bottom of the crater stood five yellow-eyed dogs, staring up at them over the bloody carcass of a goat.

Claudia grabbed Martha's arm and Martha instinctively reached for Mr. Bindar.

"Those are the guards' dogs aren't they?" she whispered, terrified by the sight of the mangy animals.

"No," Mr. Bindar whispered back. "These are feral dogs. They come out after night and scavenge. They kill what they can. People call them 'Satan wolves.'"

The dogs' ears and eyes were still fixed on the intruders. Martha listened to their growls, now low, deep rumbles in the backs of their throats.

"Will you have to shoot them?" she asked anxiously.

Mr. Bindar shook his head. "No," he whispered, "I won't shoot them unless they come after us. Their kill might keep them busy, and if I shoot, then everyone hunting us knows where we are."

Mr. Bindar pointed along the rim of the crater and motioned for Martha and Claudia to go on. "Move slowly until you are out of their sight," he said. "I make sure those filthy things don't change their mind."

When they had walked on several yards, Martha glanced over her shoulder and saw Mr. Bindar slowly backing away from the dogs, his gun at the ready. Martha and Claudia waited while he caught up and soon all three were stumbling along again in painful flight.

Just as the wash curved down into the town, Martha heard faint voices and the sounds of rocks tumbling.

"They are coming," Mr. Bindar whispered. He directed them to scramble out of the wash and onto the edge of a narrow street of featureless adobe buildings. Hurriedly, they crossed the street and ducked into a doorway. Martha's heart pounded in her ears. She caught Claudia's hands and suddenly, for just a moment, the joy of being together overwhelmed the terror of being pursued.

At the end of the street there was a little plaza. A group of men sat on flimsy folding chairs around a tin table and played cards. A small fire burned close by. Beyond the plaza, framed at the end of another narrow street, a minaret rose like a spike driven into the gloom of the night. Martha could hear the low exclamations of the men and the crackle of their little fire. The moment seemed dismally incongruous, the men enjoying a peaceful card game while she and Claudia, two lost women, were running for their lives.

Suddenly, Martha heard the dogs again, the ones they had left behind in the wash, howling. The howling didn't last long. Gunshots punctuated the night and the dogs fell silent. Martha couldn't help but imagine what grisly fate the dogs had met.

"Listen!" Mr. Bindar whispered emphatically. "There is something coming." Neither woman had to struggle to hear the car rattling loudly over the muted sounds of the night. Martha thought it sounded more like a lawn mower than a car, as it popped and whined its way closer to them. Soon its dim, vibrating headlights were visible coming up the street. It was a micro Renault, a tiny car, its paint sandblasted away in huge patches.

When the car got within fifty feet of their hiding place, Mr. Bindar pulled Martha away from Claudia and picked her up. "Do what I say," he commanded. And then, carrying her in his arms, he stepped out into the sandy street.

The little car skidded to a halt. Martha imagined what the driver was seeing: an ugly man carrying his sick wife, pleading for help in getting her to the hospital or back home.

The man rolled down his window and seemed to swell with importance. That is, until Mr. Bindar set Martha on her feet and drew his Uzi.

"We need you to drive us to the army barracks," Mr. Bindar barked, "and then you can go on your way." Before the driver could respond, Mr. Bindar signaled for Claudia to come out of the doorway.

Martha saw now that the driver was a dwarf. He sat on a cushion and his dirty head wrap was tied loosely and stacked high on top of his head. His thin face betrayed his fear.

When the driver saw Claudia approaching the car, his fright turned into protest. "You can never fit," he said. "There are too many of you. You must wait for another car." He moved to roll up his window up and dismiss them, but before he could, Mr. Bindar thrust the Uzi into the car, close to the man's face.

The voices coming from the wash behind them were louder now, words almost distinguishable. "You will take us or we will go without you, maybe leave you dead," Mr. Bindar said to the driver. "What do you think?"

The man nodded. Martha, Claudia, and then Mr. Bindar crammed into the little Renault and the car pulled away, smoking and coughing up the dark street.

A bizarrely amusing thought popped into Martha's exhausted mind as they drove away. She expected they must look a circus act, she and Claudia squeezed in the backseat like double-jointed contortionists, and in the front seat, a dwarf and an earless giant.

CHAPTER 24

The first mortar rounds hit the army barracks less than an hour after the dwarf reported that he had tricked his captors and barely escaped while they were preparing to torture and kill him with razors.

He had driven his captors the ten minutes into the mountains, to the barracks, and then back into town, the little car laying down exhaust like a smoke screen. Unwittingly, the dwarf headed right into the commotion surrounding the palace until, stopped by Price Jed al Hann's guards, he could go no further. When he told them what happened, radios cracked with excited voices, meaningless AK47 bursts where fired into the air, and groups of men, wearing robes over long pants, many of their faces too young to support full beards, some wearing head wraps or cone-shaped caps, appeared from the streets below, gathered on the palace drive, and shouted oaths while waiting for something more angry to do.

The army barracks was situated behind a Cyclone fence topped with rolls of razor wire. The barracks themselves were simply four, squat concrete buildings built against a steep rock slope. Into the rock a bunker had been built, a short tunnel, and in that tunnel a tank was kept. Just one. The rest of the tanks had been moved closer to the Libyan border, and the one left behind was an old Sheridan, no match for the Libyan rockets on the front. Eight soldiers had been left behind with it.

The barracks hadn't been shelled for many months, but there had been no attempt to repair them during the lull. They were pocked and broken, whole sections of walls blown to ragged fragments and dangling slabs of concrete. It would have been hard to tell the old damage from the new.

That night, the eight soldiers sat inside the bunker, the unexplained explosions from the outside barely audible over the music from their portable radio.

Mr. Bindar, Martha, and Claudia were not with them.

CHAPTER 25

Martha learned that Mr. Bindar had anticipated a flight to the barracks in the middle of some night, and then the immediate need to move on from the barracks to avoid being captured. The army captain who had been left behind in charge of the little platoon and their one tank was happy to help the secret police.

"The captain gets bored just sitting around day after day," Mr. Bindar explained to the women.

So, when the little Renault had deposited its passengers, the army captain immediately stowed Mr. Bindar, Martha, and Claudia in a camouflaged army pickup and took them high up towards a pass into the Tassili Plateau, as planned.

The journey was long and the way rough. Martha and Claudia could hear mortar rounds behind them, echoing off narrow rock passes. When the pickup rattled along exposed switchback turns, they could see the sparks of explosions over the sheer drops below, crystal clear in the frigid night. But more than the fear of being recaptured by Prince Jed al Hann's men, Martha and Claudia felt exhaustion.

While the woman dosed, drifting in and out of consciousness, the army captain, behind the wheel, talked with Mr. Bindar in a low, conspiratorial voice. Occasionally, one of the men issued a grunt that Martha took for a reluctant laugh. Sometimes the men smoked in silence, the tips of their foul smelling cigarettes glowing orange in the dark cab.

Claudia seemed to sink into a deeper sleep; in response, Martha came wide awake and held Claudia more tightly against her. There was nothing as far as her eye could see except rock and the weak beams of the pickup's headlights moving through narrow canyons or along precipitous ledges. Silently, Martha thanked the army captain for his superior driving skills; how the man kept their vehicle on the nearly indistinguishable track was beyond her.

After hours of grinding gears, and lurching, and bitter cold, Martha felt as if she had fallen into a particularly unpleasant trance. When the pickup finally stopped and the army captain turned off the headlights, Martha's uneasy trance exploded and she found herself almost sick with the sudden stillness and quiet.

They were on top of a plateau, out in the open. Around them were the dark shapes of low, sagging tents, maybe thirty of them. Martha had seen these before, Tuareg tents, but she had not seen them in such a forlorn place. The wind was howling, and the sides of the tents were flapping wildly, as if at any second whole sections, whole tents, would blow away.

Nothing seemed to be alive. Three huge, stake-bed trucks were parked nearby, and Martha wondered if they were abandoned, waiting for the wind or scavengers to strip them clean.

Martha and Claudia stepped out of the pickup and wearily followed Mr. Bindar to one of the tents.

"We will sleep with the Tuareg tonight," he said. "They have been waiting here for days. They will take you the rest of the way into Libya."

"And what about the captain?" Martha asked.

Mr. Bindar grunted. "He will take care of himself, be sure of it."

The night air was bitterly cold, but inside the Tuareg tent Martha and Claudia found the black comfort of animal warmth. They could barely distinguish one sleeping, snoring form from another, gathered as they were in groups of two and three under piles of rugs and heavy blankets.

Mr. Bindar immediately set to work moving somnolent bodies aside and snatching blankets until he had dug a nest for the women in the middle of the tent.

"Thank you," Martha whispered and Claudia grasped his hand. Mr. Bindar only nodded and slipped out of the tent.

ACROSS

The women curled in among the sleeping Tuareg. They held each other, first to get warm, then just because they finally could. The smells—smoke and lanolin and musk—were feral, cloying, but oddly comforting. Claudia slid her hand up inside Martha's haik. Her fingers found Martha's lovely nipple and she sighed. Here, in a Tuareg tent high in the frigid Sahara night, everything was familiar again.

CHAPTER 25

Martha bolted awake. The Tuareg woman who had roughly shaken her handed her handed a note and left the tent. The note was written in perfect French.

Mss's Bekele and Simmerhorn,

I had to travel on last night after you went to sleep. You will be safe now. Go with the Tuareg into Libya. They will give you clothes so you look like them. When they get to the town of Sardalas, they will hand you over to the Libyans who will make celebrities out of you and show the world how horrible Algeria is. They will get you home fast.

I want to say goodbye. I have all my life wanted to be exposed to something decent and lovely. It is hard in my country right now and even harder, you probably noticed, when you look like me. But because of being with you, now I have. What is in my heart is as pure as your love for each other.

With deep respect,

Abbas Bindar,

Assistant Commissioner of Police

Sovereign Republic of Algeria

CHAPTER 26

There was no wind that morning and the sky was a blue of such deep clarity that the eye was challenged to look deeply enough up into it for something else, some presence behind its unrelieved vastness.

The three truckswhich were old Mercedes,were overloaded, mushrooming with bundles and sacks and rugs and baskets and unwieldy duffels that spilled over their wood plank sides, and down to the tires. On top of these bundles the Tuareg perched, dozens per truck, their heads and dark faces swathed in indigo wraps. They balanced high on the loads, clung to ropes, and perched on teetering crates. The lucky ones made seats on sacks of grain. They were going to Libya, some farther on into Chad.

And for two of the smallest figures, huddled together in a little fort of burlap sacks of nuts on the top of a cab, much farther.

CHAPTER 27

Two months later an AP item ran in the *New York Times*, back on page twenty-seven.

Coast Guard and Bust

CHARLESTON, South Carolina—*While small by Coast Guard standards, the seizure of 125 kilograms of pure heroin yesterday in the port of Charleston, South Carolina added another troubling dimension to the difficulty of international drug interdiction, according to Commander Charles VanLamb.*

"The heroin was found on a small freighter in the cabin of a skipper who had an honorable reputation as a seaman. It seems now that we have to worry about any vessel and each and every crew member that comes into any port in U.S. waters."

The ship, the Swan II, was returning from Turkey. It was less than five miles from port when, acting on a tip, the Coast Guard boarded her. The heroin was found in the captain's cabin. "It had not even been hidden well," Commander VanLamb said. "It was obvious that the captain didn't regard U.S. laws or the U.S. Coast Guard as a threat."

The Swan II's captain, Michael Rappa, insisted that he had no knowledge of the heroin. He will be arraigned in federal court Monday.

CHAPTER 28

It was late December. The snow fell more heavily than it had all day, sticking to the trees and covering Central Park, as if adding final decorating touches for the holidays. The Christmas lights along Park Avenue shown like a million crystals in the wet night. Taxis negotiated the slippery streets, their headlights making yellow cones as they shone ahead into the curtain of snowflakes.

Martha and Claudia stood at the window of their suite in the Pierre Hotel, looking down at the hush descending over the December night. What had happened to them less than two months earlier still came back to Martha in waves of disbelief. Had there really been such a time? Could they really have survived it?

Yes, there had been such a dreadful time. And yes, together Martha and Claudia had survived it.

Standing together at the window of their hotel suite, looking down at handsome cabs and limousines and people in topcoats and furs hurrying into the hotel for dinner or holiday parties, Martha was acutely aware that the safety they owned now was something they had earned.

Martha gently squeezed Claudia's hand; Claudia squeezed Martha's in return.

For Martha, the memories of those days in search of Claudia were not entirely unpleasant. She still wore the brass and silver jewelry the Tuareg women had given her and thought of the first night she had spent with them as one of the most spiritual moments of her life.

She remembered, too, Mr. Bindar's dedication to their quest; she often recalled his making a nest for her and Claudia that last, freezing night with the Tuareg.

And she still remembered irrepressible music and joy in forlorn places.

What she didn't want to remember, but did, was Nikkos and what he suggested of the evil in the world. What she didn't want to remember but did was Claudia chained and almost naked, sitting alone on the big bed, playing Mozart.

The cello, of course, the expensive, cherished Amati, had been left behind at Prince Jed al Hann's palace. At first it made Martha furious to think of it sitting there, abandoned. It made her heart break when she thought of Claudia without it. But before long the anger and sadness had threatened to overwhelm Martha, so she had forced herself to think more hopeful, if not happy, thoughts.

Maybe, just maybe, that women who had helped them reach Claudia, Tahani, the woman carrying the prince's son, maybe she would find a good home for Claudia's cello. Maybe she would find someone to play it for her and her baby.

Martha looked out at the frosty winter night and shivered, though the hotel room was toasty and warm. It would be a long time before the bad memories ceased to chill her soul.

Claudia's tidal recollections, erased of their specificity by some mysterious process of repression, engulfed her in unpredictable waves of panic: at Lulu's, when the waiter had looked at her in a strange way; on Sacramento Street, when the van cut her off and then stopped, blocking her way while the driver made a delivery; in the taxi, when the driver took her back to the hotel by an unfamiliar route.

Even in her own home.

One morning, shortly after she and Martha had returned to the United States, Claudia lay in their familiar bed, just barely awake. She reached out for Martha, drowsily sweeping her hand across the cool silkiness of the sheets. When her hand could not find Martha, Claudia was jolted awake. Her heart racing, she called out for Martha, trying unsuccessfully to keep the terror out of her voice. But when there was no answer, Claudia fell apart. She felt more abandoned and alone than she had ever felt, completely unable to cope with a world that was so threatening and cruel. Martha returned five minutes later with the *Chronicle* and a bag of warm croissants and found Claudia curled in a ball, sobbing.

What Claudia needed was to be held, to never be far from Martha's touch again. And Martha, her own Martha, understood the care and tenderness it would take to nurture Claudia back to health.

There was one thing about her awful captivity, however, that Claudia did remember with curious, uncomfortable pleasure. The ribbons. She remembered the way she had learned to hold her hands out, wrists together, to be bound; she remembered the way the ribbons were wound, first gently and then more snugly around her wrists. Finally, she remembered how by the time the knot was tied and finished off with an intricate bow, she had felt a curious abandon, as if she had been excused from the responsibilities of the world.

Except for Tahani Claudia had, of course, despised her captors. But as she thought more and more about her captivity since being reunited with Martha, the ribbons and the utter helplessness of being so secured, were recollections of disturbing comfort.

The snow had turned into a blizzard, the lights and movement below veiled and stilled. It was still early but it was time for bed.

Claudia watched as Martha undid the curtain ties, allowing the heavy brocade drapes to fall across the window. After pulling the two sides together, Martha went into the bedroom to turn down their bed. When she returned to the living room a few moments later, Claudia still stood where she had been, as if somehow looking through the curtains and out the window.

But Claudia was staring at the curtain tie, at the silken, tasseled cord. Then, tentatively, she reached out and touched the cord. And then, she removed it from its brass bracket and wound the cord loosely around one wrist, as if testing its suppleness.

Claudia knew that Martha was watching her. She turned and offered the cord to Martha. Then she slipped off her silk robe, letting it fall around her feet where it became a patch of pure blue ice.

She looked directly up into Martha's eyes for a moment, asking for something, and then looked down, ashamed by what she was asking. She held her hands out, wrists together, and waited.

When Martha had completed her task, she led Claudia into the bedroom, gently pulling on the tassel end of the tie. She helped Claudia get up and into the bed, and then, after turning off the light, pulled the covers up over them both. She rolled Claudia onto her side, and then curled up against her, hugging her from behind.

Claudia felt Martha's warmth, her strength, her magnificent, powerful hands, and her own wonderful helplessness. She drifted into an ecstasy of well-being and finally into sleep, completely safe from the world.

ABOUT THE AUTHOR

Blue Dawson is a professor of English and a legislative advocate. She punctuates her teaching schedule and legislative committee meetings by traveling throughout the world, sometimes into its most restive countries. She considers herself not a tourist but a traveler.

She has written numerous publications on educational policy. Additionally, she writes short stories and poetry. She is presently working on a novel about Peru.

LETTER TO THE READER

I hope you have enjoyed *Across*. I wanted to write a story about loyalty and the despair of separation, and I wanted to write a story about the paradox of the libido, how for some it expresses itself as tenderness but for others, the dark opposite, violence.

I also wanted to write a story about wonderful places and wonderful people very far away. I chose North Africa for the setting of this novel since its stark landscape so dramatically creates and illuminates character, both good and bad. My next book will take place in the Andes of Ecuador, an immensely different landscape that carves characters as wonderfully and as ruthlessly as the Sahara did in Across.

ACROSS

2005 Publication Schedule

January

A Heart's Awakening
Veronica Parker
$9.95
1-58571-143-8

Falling
Natalie Dunbar
$9.95
1-58571-121-7

February

Echoes of Yesterday
Beverly Clark
$9.95
1-58571-131-4

A Love of Her Own
Cheris F. Hodges
$9.95
1-58571-136-5

Higher Ground
Leah Latimer
$19.95
1-58571-157-8

March

Misconceptions
Pamela Leigh Starr
$9.95
1-58571-117-9

I'll Paint a Sun
A.J. Garrotto
$9.95
1-58571-165-9

Peace Be Still
Colette Haywood
$12.95
1-58571-129-2

April

Intentional Mistakes
Michele Sudler
$9.95
1-58571-152-7

Conquering Dr. Wexler's Heart
Kimberley White
$9.95
1-58571-126-8

Song in the Park
Martin Brant
$15.95
1-58571-125-X

May

The Color Line
Lizzette Grayson Carter
$9.95
1-58571-163-2

Unconditional
A.C. Arthur
$9.95
1-58571-142-X

Last Train to Memphis
Elsa Cook
$12.95
1-58571-146-2

June

Angel's Paradise
Janice Angelique
$9.95
1-58571-107-1

Suddenly You
Crystal Hubbard
$9.95
1-58571-158-6

Matters of Life and
    Death
Lesego Malepe, Ph.D.
$15.95
1-58571-124-1

2005 Publication Schedule (continued)

July

Class Reunion
Irma Jenkins/John
  Brown
$12.95
1-58571-123-3

Wild Ravens
Altonya Washington
$9.95
1-58571-164-0

August

Path of Thorns
Annetta P. Lee
$9.95
1-58571-145-4

Timeless Devotion
Bella McFarland
$9.95
1-58571-148-9

Life Is Never As It Seems
J.J. Michael
$12.95
1-58571-153-5

September

Beyond Rapture
Beverly Clark
$9.95
1-58571-130-6

Blood Lust
J. M. Jeffries
$9.95
1-58571-138-1

Rough on Rats and
  Tough on Cats
Chris Parker
$12.95
1-58571-154-3

October

A Will to Love
Angie Daniels
$9.95
1-58571-141-1

Taken by You
Dorothy Elizabeth Love
$9.95
1-58571-162-4

Soul Eyes
Wayne L. Wilson
$12.95
1-58571-147-0

November

A Drummer's Beat to
  Mend
Kei Swanson
$9.95
1-58571-171-3

Sweet Reprecussions
Kimberley White
$9.95
1-58571-159-4

Red Polka Dot in a
  World of Plaid
Varian Johnson
$12.95
1-58571-140-3

December

Hand in Glove
Andrea Jackson
$9.95
1-58571-166-7

Blaze
Barbara Keaton
$9.95
1-58571-172-1

Across
Blue Dawson
$12.95
1-58571-149-7

Other Genesis Press, Inc. Titles

Erotic Anthology	Assorted	$8.95
Eve's Prescription	Edwina Martin Arnold	$8.95
Everlastin' Love	Gay G. Gunn	$8.95
Fate	Pamela Leigh Starr	$8.95
Forbidden Quest	Dar Tomlinson	$10.95
Fragment in the Sand	Annetta P. Lee	$8.95
From the Ashes	Kathleen Suzanne	$8.95
	Jeanne Sumerix	
Gentle Yearning	Rochelle Alers	$10.95
Glory of Love	Sinclair LeBeau	$10.95
Hart & Soul	Angie Daniels	$8.95
Heartbeat	Stephanie Bedwell-Grime	$8.95
I'll Be Your Shelter	Giselle Carmichael	$8.95
Illusions	Pamela Leigh Starr	$8.95
Indiscretions	Donna Hill	$8.95
Interlude	Donna Hill	$8.95
Intimate Intentions	Angie Daniels	$8.95
Just an Affair	Eugenia O'Neal	$8.95
Kiss or Keep	Debra Phillips	$8.95
Love Always	Mildred E. Riley	$10.95
Love Unveiled	Gloria Greene	$10.95
Love's Deception	Charlene Berry	$10.95
Mae's Promise	Melody Walcott	$8.95
Meant to Be	Jeanne Sumerix	$8.95
Midnight Clear	Leslie Esdaile	$10.95
(Anthology)	Gwynne Forster	
	Carmen Green	
	Monica Jackson	
Midnight Magic	Gwynne Forster	$8.95
Midnight Peril	Vicki Andrews	$10.95
My Buffalo Soldier	Barbara B. K. Reeves	$8.95
Naked Soul	Gwynne Forster	$8.95
No Regrets	Mildred E. Riley	$8.95
Nowhere to Run	Gay G. Gunn	$10.95

ACROSS

Object of His Desire	A. C. Arthur	$8.95
One Day at a Time	Bella McFarland	$8.95
Passion	T.T. Henderson	$10.95
Past Promises	Jahmel West	$8.95
Path of Fire	T.T. Henderson	$8.95
Picture Perfect	Reon Carter	$8.95
Pride & Joi	Gay G. Gunn	$8.95
Quiet Storm	Donna Hill	$8.95
Reckless Surrender	Rochelle Alers	$8.95
Rendezvous with Fate	Jeanne Sumerix	$8.95
Revelations	Cheris F. Hodges	$8.95
Rivers of the Soul	Leslie Esdaile	$8.95
Rooms of the Heart	Donna Hill	$8.95
Shades of Brown	Denise Becker	$8.95
Shades of Desire	Monica White	$8.95
Sin	Crystal Rhodes	$8.95
So Amazing	Sinclair LeBeau	$8.95
Somebody's Someone	Sinclair LeBeau	$8.95
Someone to Love	Alicia Wiggins	$8.95
Soul to Soul	Donna Hill	$8.95
Still Waters Run Deep	Leslie Esdaile	$8.95
Subtle Secrets	Wanda Y. Thomas	$8.95
Sweet Tomorrows	Kimberly White	$8.95
The Color of Trouble	Dyanne Davis	$8.95
The Price of Love	Sinclair LeBeau	$8.95
The Reluctant Captive	Joyce Jackson	$8.95
The Missing Link	Charlyne Dickerson	$8.95
Three Wishes	Seressia Glass	$8.95
Tomorrow's Promise	Leslie Esdaile	$8.95
Truly Inseperable	Wanda Y. Thomas	$8.95
Twist of Fate	Beverly Clark	$8.95
Unbreak My Heart	Dar Tomlinson	$8.95
Unconditional Love	Alicia Wiggins	$8.95
When Dreams A Float	Dorothy Elizabeth Love	$8.95

Whispers in the Night	Dorothy Elizabeth Love	$8.95
Whispers in the Sand	LaFlorya Gauthier	$10.95
Yesterday is Gone	Beverly Clark	$8.95
Yesterday's Dreams, Tomorrow's Promises	Reon Laudat	$8.95
Your Precious Love	Sinclair LeBeau	$8.95

Order Form

Mail to: Genesis Press, Inc.
P.O. Box 101
Columbus, MS 39703

Name _____

Address _____

City/State _____ Zip _____

Telephone _____

Ship to (if different from above)

Name _____

Address _____

City/State _____ Zip _____

Telephone _____

Credit Card Information

Credit Card # _____ ☐ Visa ☐ Mastercard

Expiration Date (mm/yy) _____ ☐ AmEx ☐ Discover

Qty.	Author	Title	Price	Total

Use this order

form, or call

1-888-INDIGO-1

Total for books _____

Shipping and handling:
  $5 first two books,
  $1 each additional book _____

Total S & H _____

Total amount enclosed _____

Mississippi residents add 7% sales tax